Tom Fletcher
and the
Three Wise Men

Tom Fletcher
and the
Three Wise Men

Sarah Matthias

For Emma Neely,
with love

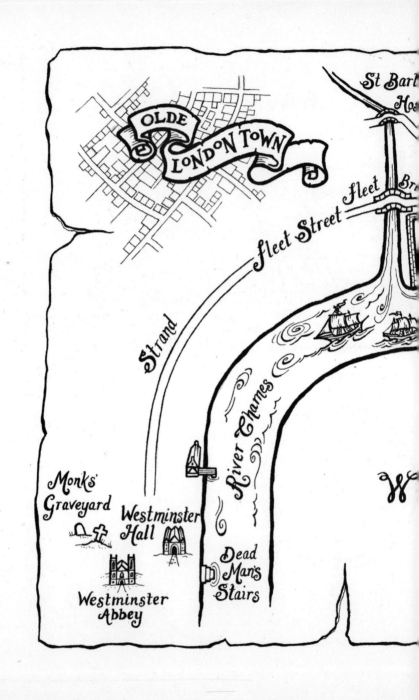

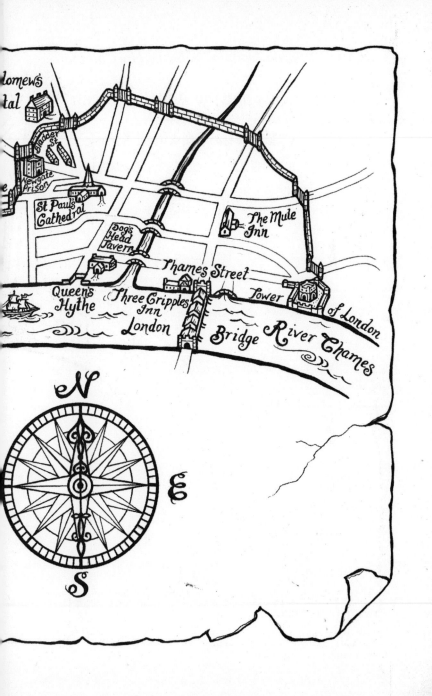

Also by Sarah Matthias published by Catnip

Tom Fletcher and the Angel of Death

The Riddle of the Poisoned Monk

CATNIP BOOKS

Published by Catnip Publishing Ltd

14 Greville Street

London EC1N 8SB

First published 2009

1 3 5 7 9 10 8 6 4 2

Text copyright © Sarah Matthias 2009

Map copyright © Sally Taylor 2009

The moral right of the author has been asserted

All rights reserved

A CIP catalogue record for this book is available from the British Library

ISBN 978-1-84647-069-1

Printed in Poland

www.catnippublishing.co.uk

Contents

List of Characters:

The Novices

Tom Fletcher	chief novice – son of a local arrow maker
Herbert Glanville	novice – son of a local corn merchant
Edmund	youngest novice – orphan
Felix	a novice
Odo	a novice

The Monks

Abbot Fergus	Abbot of Saint Wilfred's Abbey
Brother Dunstan	Novice Master
Brother Ambrose	Quill Master
Brother Ethelwig	Inventor and Keeper of the Bell Tower
Brother Silas	Physician

Townspeople of Saint Agnes Next-the-Sea

Gabriel Miller	miller
Alice Miller	his wife
Bessie Miller	their daughter
Abigail Abrahams	Bessie's best friend
Sir Ranulf de Lacy	Lord of Micklow Manor
Fustian	Clerk to Sir Ranulf de Lacy
Baron Godric de Mordon	Bessie's suitor
Job Pug	Belfry assistant
Mistress Job	his wife

London

Abbot Swithin	Abbot of Westminster Abbey
Brother Gideon	Sacrist of Westminster Abbey
Sir Henry de Mandeville	Lord Chief Justice of England
Mabel de Mandeville	his daughter
Sir Percy FitzNigel	The King's Justice
Humphrey Pickerel	servant to Sir Percy
Jocelyn de Maltby	a knight
Bartholomew Bucket	Tom's friend
Flea	a mongrel

Prologue

The Golden Casket
Cairo and London – 1220

Crocodile Tears

J ocelyn de Maltby flexed his silver finger. It throbbed in the heat of the Cairo sun, the metal too tight around the tender stump – all that remained of the once elegant first digit of his right hand. And yet he had reason to be grateful. The Nile crocodile had kindly left him a sizeable lump of flesh and the good doctors of Egypt had fashioned a fine replacement for the piece of bone and gristle that had strayed too close to the reptile's grinning jaws. The finger sparkled in a shaft of sunlight. The craftsmanship was exquisite, de Maltby had to admit. And yet it really was too bad for a brave crusader, who had outwitted death in battle, to lose a careless finger to the jaws of a hungry crocodile.

'But de Maltby always has the last laugh,' he muttered to himself with a grim smile, stroking the knobbly leather of his crocodile-skin bag.

With a nervous glance around the room, Sir Jocelyn

looped the silken cord of the bag around his neck. And then with his hand on his dagger, he used its wicked point to press aside the drapery that covered the doorway of the crumbling old house in the shadow of the Zuweila gate. He peered, wary as a fox, up and down the bustling warren of the Cairo bazaar, narrowing his eyes against the smoky fug that billowed from the crackling spits of sizzling goat and flat pans of roasting locusts.

And certainly, there was more than a little of the fox about Jocelyn de Maltby, with his sly amber eyes and curling beard, the colour of palest copper. But as he slipped stealthily into the secret heart of the ancient city, who would have guessed that the auburn hair, hidden beneath the thick dark hood was cut for a soldier's helmet? No one, except perhaps the black-eyed lemon seller, who seemed to pause in the inky shadows as Sir Jocelyn paused, and emerge again into the sunlight as Sir Jocelyn moved swiftly on.

But the roar of the battlefield was far from the knight's thoughts as he plunged through the babble of foreign tongues and the sharp *tap*! *tap*! of the copper engraver's hammer. Skirting the shimmering fountain at the edge of the spice bazaar, he flung an anxious backward glance over the sea of crimson turbans, baggy pantaloons and swaying camels. Was he being followed? He narrowed his eyes. *Surely he had seen that lemon-seller before, with the mark on his forehead – like a brand in the shape of a flame.* With a snarl of annoyance, he pressed his lean body into a doorway to allow a flock of fat-tailed sheep to wobble past. The lemon-seller paused too, resting his basket on a wine barrel, and following on again as de Maltby ducked furtively behind a stall of golden onions.

Deep in the tangled labyrinth of covered alleyways, a Cairo perfume-maker clicked his worry beads with mounting impatience, his agitated thumb moving rapidly to and fro across the smooth round eggs of ebony and ivory. *Would the soldier never come? And if he did – would he bring a fitting price?* Beads of sweat glistened in the plump creases of his face as he stared at the lumpy object on the table in front of him, concealed beneath a crimson cloth. Perhaps he had been foolish to trust the sandy-whiskered Englishman. After all, his tongue was too red and his teeth too sharp.

The perfume-maker swallowed a lump in his throat. The rhythmic clack of the beads had failed to work their usual magic. For days now he had sensed he was being watched; a glimpse of a cinnamon robe beyond the window of his little shop, the glint of an eye at his keyhole – and he'd slept at night with a hand on his knife. But today he knew it for sure. Pots of costly frankincense lay shattered on the sandy floor, amongst the broken fragments of a jar of spikenard – the tell-tale remains of unwelcome guests. He felt sure the intruders were not searching for cinnamon oil, or a paste of ginger-grass against the stinking of the breath . . .

He spun round with a cry of alarm, his worry beads clattering to the ground. But it was not an assassin's knife in the dark. It was the knight – come at last; the soldier with the crocodile-skin bag.

5

* * *

The Cairo perfume-maker slipped the damask cloth from the golden casket that lay on the table between them. Jocelyn de Maltby caught his breath. The coffer was not large, barely the size of a kitten, inlaid with tiny silver flames that shone with a strange brightness. And wound around the middle of the box was a many-stranded cord of purest lamb's wool, three knots along its length and ending in a moonstone, shaped to resemble a teardrop. De Maltby seized it hungrily, his eyes greedy with desire.

'Not so fast, white man!' hissed the merchant, his finger still coiled around the coffer's silken cord. 'You are not the only one who seeks the casket.' He jerked a meaningful thumb towards the tumble of broken jars on the floor. 'And that must increase the price.'

Sir Jocelyn tipped up the crocodile-skin bag. The golden coins rushed from its gaping mouth, rolling and spinning onto the table between them, more and more and still they came, clinking and whispering, an endless stream of gold, until the final coin dropped with a clatter and at last the bag was empty. And now it was the merchant's eyes that burned with greed. He knew precisely what the casket was, and why this pale-faced Christian would pay so rich a price. He had felt not a moment's peace since he'd come by the pretty chest – and now he could not wait to be rid of it.

Jocelyn de Maltby licked his lips with a pointed tongue, eyes on the trader's finger as it slowly uncoiled itself from around the glowing ornament. 'Is it a deal?' he hissed, unable to disguise the tremor in his voice.

The trader chuckled. 'It is a deal, you mad Englishman!'

he cried, raking the glittering coins towards him with both plump hands.

Jocelyn de Maltby's shoulders relaxed. He was sweating, although the shadowy shop was cool. He lifted the casket from the table, cradling it for a moment in the crook of his arm, before placing it in the bag where the golden coins had been. Then, with his hand once more on the hilt of his dagger, he vanished into the bazaar, before the trader could change his mind.

But Sir Jocelyn need not have feared. For in the dim shadows of the Cairo perfume shop, amongst the aromas of frankincense and myrrh, the old man cracked his knuckles with a satisfied grin. Like de Maltby and the crocodile – he knew which one of them had made the better deal.

Indeed, as Sir Jocelyn de Maltby wove through the hubbub of the slave market, ducking stealthily through the silver bazaar, he glanced uneasily over his shoulder. He was being followed again, he was certain of it . . . by the delicate scent of lemons.

Dead Man's Stairs

There was thick snow in the fields around Westminster Abbey and the wild geese had flown, rising in a clamour of wings, seeking the warmer fields to the west. The wind was in the east and Abbot Swithin's thin nose was an icicle as it poked above the thick fur mantle that covered his bed. The icicle jumped in sudden alarm. A frenzied banging on the door rattled the flares on the cold stone wall, disturbing the sleepy occupant hunched under a mound of furs. The old man's breath was smoke as he wriggled the yellow soles of his feet into his sable slippers and shuffled across the rushes as the frantic hammering shook the door to its hinges. The watchman's voice was shrill. 'In the name of God, open up! There's a body! Under the ice. At the foot of Dead Man's Stairs!'

The icicle sniffed in irritation, the fingers of its owner fumbling with the iron latch. Abbot Swithin knew all about Dead Man's Stairs, on the great bow bend of the treacherous

River Thames, where the bodies of the drowned seemed to congregate for some reason best known to themselves. Who had not heard of that sinister place? Abbot Swithin could see the evil steps in his mind's eye, slick with dark weed, and the rats sharpening their teeth on dead men's bones. But why wake a tired old man from his bed this bleak midwinter's night? Everyone knew the Thames was as greedy as the merchants who plied their trade along its banks, sucking victims of crime or desperate souls into its grimy underbelly. The lucky ones reached the estuary, floating out to sea on the ebb tide. But there were always a few poor wretches that refused to sink . . . and bobbed back up again at Dead Man's Stairs.

The anxious watchman's boots rang hollow across the frosty cloisters of the great abbey where the bones of Edward the Confessor lay. He was holding his storm lantern aloft, lighting the abbot's path, thankful for the freezing weather that turned the rutted, filthy mud to iron. The abbot bent his skinny back into the biting wind. His lips were purple with cold as he scurried after the watchman, knees creaking in sympathy with the icy puddles, down through the warren of narrow alleyways that led to the water gate.

There was something rotten at the foot of Dead Man's Stairs amongst the ooze and slime. Hunched like a heron, the abbot stooped, peering anxiously into the pool at the bottom of the crumbling steps. A rat scampered down the bank, slithered through the fragile ice and was swallowed by the blackness beyond the circle of lantern light. The abbot's breath whistled like broken bagpipes as he stared in horror of recognition at the bloated body bumping softly against the bank.

'Careful! I . . . I wouldn't if I was you,' stammered the watchman, as the old man began to pick his way down the slippery steps. 'We don't want two corpses for the price of one!' Perhaps he had been over hasty. Maybe he should have waited until dawn to break the news of the body of the monk to the Abbot of Westminster Abbey. 'It's strange,' called the watchman, 'for a monk to do himself in. He'll be damned to hell fire in the devil's own cauldron!'

But the abbot was too busy with the corpse of Brother Gideon to reply. He tugged at a snake of grey-green weed that seemed to have coiled, like a necklace, around the swollen neck. The weed slithered free revealing a horizontal mark that gleamed blue-black on the monk's throat. The abbot stared in bewilderment at the slimy cord in his hand, as beads of river water formed like pearls along its length, and plopped into the choppy water at his feet. Painfully, he began to mount the stairs. 'Suicide?' he muttered. 'A man cannot throttle himself, I think.'

The rope he clutched was many stranded. Three knots along its length. The river had stained the white strands grey, but . . . *What was this, dangling from the end of the cord?* The abbot turned the object gently between his thumb and for efinger. It was a gem, the colour of quicksilver, with the light of the stars behind it. A moonstone, fashioned into the shape of a tear.

The New Privy

S ir Percy FitzNigel, King's Justice, sat on the fashionable privy in his new stone house near the Palace of Westminster, two miles upstream from the thieves' alleys and filthy streets of the City of London. His teeth chattered but his spirits were high, in spite of the freezing weather.

'Oh my love has golden hair
Fa la la la la!
A waist so slender, skin so fair
Tra la la la la!' warbled the lawyer, rolling his cow's eyes in ecstasy at the memory of the rosebud lips of Mabel de Mandeville, the Chief Justice's luscious daughter.

He shuddered, puckering his fleshy lips over prominent front teeth and began to struggle back into his embroidered britches with their squirrel linings. *Oh but it was chilly! Heaven be praised for an indoor privy with a padded cushion!* Sir Percy smiled smugly. It was rumoured the

King had a latrine of polished marble in the Palace of Westminster, so why not Sir Percy FitzNigel, a ruthless young lawyer, whose designs on the Chief Justice's comely daughter were second only to his designs on the post of Chief Justice itself?

Ambitious Sir Percy had risen fast, along with his grand stone hall with its fine windows of costly glass; one of the many that had sprung up to adorn the waterfront of this gracious bend in the River Thames. Westminster was the most fashionable of districts, the home of the clever men – bishops and lawyers, merchants and knights – and as far away as Sir Percy could wish from his former dingy lodgings off Bladder Street, with its open sewers clogged with offal and stinking of fish heads. But those ragged days were long forgotten and now the green river flowed under his sumptuous casement, although today the Thames was freezing, from Lambeth Palace to Thorney Island, and there was ice on the inside of the glass.

Sir Percy burst from his privy in a dazzling display of silk and ermine. 'Bank up the fire with brushwood, Porpoise!' he rapped to the pasty young servant who warmed his raw pink hands at a candle flame. 'And take care that it doesn't smoke.'

The sharp-nosed boy shivered in his threadbare tunic. 'The name is *Pickerel*, Sir Percy. *Humphrey Pickerel*,' he corrected, his tone as frosty as the air between them.

Sir Percy reeled back in mock regret, and then sprang towards the humble servant, his eel-like neck extended. 'Porpoise, Pilchard, Perch!' he spat, contempt in his cruel green eyes. 'You'll answer to whatever fishy name I choose.

Remember, I am paying you tuppence a day! I had enough of such impudence from my last man, Fustian, may he rot in hell! And I don't propose to put up with it from you!'

Humphrey Pickerel turned sullenly to the hearth, where Sir Percy's elegant greyhound lay stretched on a fur rug, licking its paws. The servant narrowed his hard little eyes against the glare, imagining the branches were Sir Percy as he began to thrust them violently into the flames. Sir Percy had turned to the window and was now rubbing a vigorous hole in the frosty glass with his ermine sleeve.

'Anything else, Sir Percy?' asked Pickerel, dipping an exaggerated bow to his master's back.

'Indeed there is, Stickleback,' he replied with a frown, peering down into the courtyard below. 'You can fetch another goblet and be quick about it. We have a visitor at FitzNigel Hall. The Abbot of Westminster himself if my eyes do not deceive me. Now what can he want so early in the day?'

Abbot Swithin's winter boots were no match for the December morning as he crunched towards the iron-bound door of FitzNigel Hall, marking hasty tracks in the flawless surface of the snow. He paused, grasping the boar's head knocker with painful blue fingers and gazed around at the grand half-finished courtyard with its mounds of abandoned masons' tools, frozen fountains, stables and barns, buried beneath a dazzling blanket of snow. He sniffed in disapproval. *Such extravagance! How could Sir Percy afford such a home? He was hardly the Chief Justice when all was said and done.* The abbot clicked his teeth and banged the unfortunate boar's head three times on the door.

A few moments later and Abbot Swithin was steaming in front of Sir Percy's hearth, flakes of melting snow trickling down his ankles and gathering wetly around his toes. On a table between the abbot and the lawyer, inlaid with the new FitzNigel coat of arms, lay a thrice-knotted coil of grey-green cord.

'I have told you already, Sir Percy,' protested the elderly abbot, gripping the edge of the table. 'Suicide is quite out of the question. Brother Gideon was sacrist of Westminster Abbey. A monk would never risk hell-fire and damnation by drowning himself in the Thames! Examine the corpse yourself. He was savagely throttled, I tell you. And besides, there were stones in his robes.'

Sir Percy yawned rudely. 'The stones in his robes prove my point,' he drawled. 'The wretch was desperate. Determined to sink deep into the river's slime. And that must be the end of the matter. If you insist on crying murder, then by all means raise the alarm. Inform the city authorities. If you discover the culprit I'll be happy to string him up at Smithfield and slit his nose for good measure. But more than that, I cannot do. Why, only one murderer in a hundred is ever discovered in this city!' He reached for his cloak. 'Now, I have a busy day ahead of me in Westminster Hall. The Chief Justice is indisposed again – a touch of his old tummy trouble – and I must deal with all his work: wandering hogs, butchers dumping entrails in the public latrine.' He flung his cloak around his shoulders with a flourish. 'Pilchard!' he brayed. 'Stop goggling over there like a landed fish and show Abbot Swithin the door.'

But the Abbot of Westminster's eyes were wide with indignation, two bright points of colour burning on his cheeks. He would not be dismissed by a pompous upstart in scarlet leggings! 'You may rest assured, Sir Percy,' he said testily, 'that I would not have bothered you if there had been anyone else around. However, the Sheriff of London is in the country for Christmas and, as you say, the Lord Chief Justice is unwell. So I am afraid you must hear me out,' he insisted, 'for there is something else which I believe will convince you that I speak the truth. Our precious new relic is missing – the one poor Brother Gideon obtained for the abbey. It has vanished without trace.'

Sir Percy raised a bored eyebrow. 'And what new relic is this?'

Abbot Swithin glanced warily at the pale young servant but Pickerel was engulfed in clouds of smoke, busily prodding the fire with a poker. 'A unique new relic which was to be revealed to the faithful on Christmas Day. A relic to rival the bones of Saint Thomas at Canterbury!' He leaned towards Sir Percy and whispered his ear.

Sir Percy gasped in feigned surprise and then his high-pitched laugh rang out, rattling the goblets and setting the wine a-tremble. 'God's teeth man!' he hooted. 'Isn't Edward the Confessor enough for you monks? Why, his bones draw lepers and madmen for miles around. Do we need *more* relics? Your lepers are a damned unpleasant sight. And Westminster is such a fashionable district.'

Abbot Swithin sucked in his breath. 'We have been losing pilgrims to Canterbury these last few years like fleas leaving a dying dog,' he explained, his patience stretched thin. 'Our bbey needs a new relic to rival the tomb of Saint Thomas Becket . . . and at last we had found one. This was no commonplace fragment – no ancient toe-bone or phial of the virgin's tears. Believe me, Sir Percy; this relic would have transformed our fortunes overnight. Brother Gideon had charge of it until Christmas Day. But he is dead – and the golden casket is gone!'

The Justice shrugged, pursing his mouth into a pout. 'Pray tell me,' he said fumbling with the clasp on his cloak and preparing to depart. 'What makes you so sure of a connection between the death of Brother Gideon and the disappearance of this relic?'

Abbot Swithin's face was dancing fire and shadow in the light of the crackling fire. 'Brother Gideon was in fear of his life,' he replied softly. 'He thought he was being followed – just the glint of an eye at a keyhole, the echo of a footfall at his door. He had known not a moment's peace since he had come by the relic.' He paused. 'And there was something else too. He was troubled by an unusual scent. It was something exotic . . . I believe he said it was a curious smell that reminded him of lemons.'

Part One

Saint Agnes Next-the-Sea
Yuletide

Chapter 1

The Great Bustard

The first weeks of December had touched Saint
Wilfred's with the gentlest of fingers. The early
snows had melted on the sun-warmed pinnacles
of the fairytale roofscape of the abbey and the frost lay
only faintly in the creases of the gargoyles' leering grins.
The old boar was freshly killed amidst a deal of blood and
squealing, the grapes were pressed, the oat crocks full and
there was salt-fish in the winter barrels. Little wonder there
was rejoicing in the coastal town of Saint Agnes Next-the-
Sea and at the large sandstone abbey, nestling snugly in the
valley of the River Twist. Besides it was Yuletide – a time
for feasts and merriment, red candles and mistletoe – and
the monks were in the mood for a celebration as Christmas
approached.

And they had good cause for rejoicing after the turmoil
of the summer just past, when Tom Fletcher, the most
reluctant novice in the abbey, had proved better at solving

grisly murders than learning his Latin prayers. Three months had now passed since the terrible fire when the bell tower had exploded like a fire cracker and gargoyles had poured down like stone rain. Three months had slipped by since they had dismantled the Beast House, and Delilah, the lioness, had been sent to join the King's menagerie in the Tower of London.

It was only December, yet as the bare winter branches scored the sky, a new tower, taller even than the last, had begun to sprout from the mess of rubble in its rickety cage of scaffolding and Brother Ethelwig was tying the final flight feathers to the tail of his extravagant new flying machine. And there was even better news at the abbey than the impressive new bell tower. Saint Wilfred's had a new abbot, lately installed by the Bishop in London. A Scottish dancing teacher with a melodious tenor voice and a riotous red beard. It was Brother Fergus – the most popular monk in the abbey. And they were expecting his return from the City of London this very evening – the day before Christmas Eve.

Even Brother Dunstan seemed pleased. In fact the sly little novice master's memory appeared even shorter than his temper. So that with a simple hitch of his robes to the knee in imitation of Brother Fergus, he was ready to transfer his entire devotion to the new abbot. And after dying his grey beard red with crushed madder roots, he had begun to practise musical scales in a thin reedy voice and to scold the mischievous novices in a distinctly Scottish accent.

All should have been well at Saint Wilfred's Abbey, so why was Tom Fletcher's face as long as a yuletide fiddle?

It was true that the wind had changed. The weather had caught a sudden chill, and for two days now, cross-winds from the Low Countries had howled around the abbey like the devil's own hunt. But there were blazing fires in the wide stone hearths and squirrel-lined boots for the monks and yet still Tom's spirits were as heavy as the snow that shrouded the festive Yule log in a dazzling mantle of white.

On the day before Christmas Eve and as the milky sun sank below the high hedges, Tom Fletcher leaned his shoulder into the trunk of an enormous Yule log and began the final push through the fog across the outer court of the abbey towards the great bronze doors of Saint Wilfred's.

'Come on weaklings,' urged Tom. 'Put some guts into it everyone! We're nearly there. One, two, three . . . pushhh!'

'Careful, Tom!' snapped Brother Felix. 'You trod on my heel!'

'Ouch!' Tom yelped and sucked hard on his finger. 'Another splinter! My hands are as prickly as a hedgepig's bum!'

Felix pinched his lips into a pious blue line. 'It's the same for everybody, Tom. You just moan more than anyone else, that's all.' He pulled at the rags around his chapped knuckles. 'As chief novice, you should set an example. We're all in the same pickle barrel.'

'You've got the wrong attitude, Tom,' came a pompous little voice from behind a mountain of red-eyed holly. 'I always find a prayer helps when I'm doing something I don't like. Especially now I'm preparing to take my vows. You should try it.'

Tom shot the holly a poisonous glance. 'Shut up, Odo! I'm not taking my vows on Christmas Day! I've told Brother Dunstan. Nobody can make me. I mean to talk to Brother Fer . . . I mean *Abbot* Fergus just as soon as he gets back from London. He should be here by tonight.'

A wedge of bright light expanded across the snow and a delicious draught of spicy air wafted through the kitchen shutters, followed by a shining face, dripping with perspiration. It was plump Brother Herbert – Tom's best friend.

'There he is, the lazy lump!' grumbled Tom indignantly. 'I wondered where he'd got to. Don't worry about helping with the Yule log, Herbert!' he called out sarcastically.

'Hello, Herbert! What's cooking?' called a miniature novice with golden curls, almost lost amidst a cloud of waxy mistletoe. 'Smells delicious!' The young novice licked the stubs of his two front teeth that were just emerging through his pale pink gums.

Herbert leaned out through the rectangle of light, peering at the ghostly phantoms emerging from the mist. 'It's a great bustard, Ed. It's as big as a dog and stuffed full of eels . . . and its beak will spout fire like a phoenix. Ethelwig's trying it now!'

'You're going to burst before Christmas Day, if you're not careful,' shouted Tom irritably. 'What are you doing in the kitchen, anyway?'

Herbert patted his belly. 'They know where my talents lie! Anyway, you lot had better get your skates on. It's almost time for the play rehearsal and Brother Dunstan wants us in our costumes.'

Inside the sweltering kitchen, Brother Ethelwig, ancient Keeper of the Bell Tower and eccentric inventor was turning his talents to the great bustard, busily stuffing a brandy-soaked rag into its gaping bill. 'Was that young Tom out there?' he asked, lighting a taper from the roaring fire.

'Yes,' frowned Herbert. He clicked the lattice shutter back in place. 'With a face as long as a poker. I've told him there's no point complaining. I'm taking my vows on Christmas Day too.'

Ethelwig nodded. 'You've both turned fourteen and there's no putting it off any longer.' He held the smouldering taper above the bustard's whiskery beak. 'Now, let's try this again *without* setting fire to my eyebrows!'

Herbert sighed. He just didn't understand Tom's problem. It was a good life at Saint Wilfred's, especially now Abbot Fergus was going to be in charge. Tom didn't know when he was well off. He shook his head sadly. It was quite true that Tom had never wanted to become a monk, but he'd been worse since he'd met Bessie Miller! Herbert blew out his cheeks. Bessie was all right, he supposed. But Tom seemed to think of nothing else . . .

The great bustard's beak burst suddenly into flames with a small pop as the wad of flaming linen shot from its mouth and landed in a bubbling stockpot with a fizz. 'Hooray!' cried Ethelwig. 'A bit more black powder and we'll make a firebird of it yet! What's the matter, Herbert? Aren't you impressed?'

Herbert fished the charred linen out of the pot with a ladle. The bustard and its flaming beak had suddenly lost its charm. 'Tom's a fool,' he said peevishly. 'Does he *really* think he could be a wool merchant? A poor boy like him without a penny? It's all Bessie Miller's fault. It's been Bessie-this and Bessie-that ever since the summer. He's hardly thought of anything else.'

'Any*one* else, you mean,' said Brother Ethelwig, with a sympathetic smile. 'I think someone's hurt your feelings.'

Out in the frozen court the boys had finally reached the abbey door with the Yule log, leaving a great black scar across the immaculate snow behind. The huge trunk would blaze for twelve days from Christmas Eve, kindled from a piece of wood from last year's burning, to preserve the luck of the house.

'It didn't help much this year,' said Tom gloomily, rubbing his frozen arms. He leant his aching back against the cold bronze doors and closed his eyes. He'd never felt more miserable in his life. In fact, he was desperate. Herbert was right. It *was* the black-eyed miller's daughter that was causing the hollow ache in Tom's stomach every morning. He gazed in despair at his ankles, emerging from beneath his habit; his legs had stretched through the summer like weeds in sunlight and his novice's robes felt as tight as a winding sheet.

The time really had come to take his vows.

He swallowed a lump of self-pity. Things were looking black. Worse even than that desolate day seven years ago, when kicking and screaming he was abandoned at Saint Wilfred's – one mouth too many for his hungry father to feed. Tom had always dreamed he'd escape from the abbey, on a trading vessel bound for Flanders, with a cargo of wool and the wind in his hair. But now he realised that the clattering looms were only a fool's idle dream. He had no money and no trade. So it really was all over. In two days time he would take his vows and become a real monk – cast off his dreams along with his shrunken novice's robe. And what then? Poverty, Chastity and Obedience – from Christmas Day and on into a bleak and dismal future.

And as if the prospect of taking his vows on Christmas Day were not trouble enough for an unwilling fourteen-year-old novice, there was something else too. He had just heard some dreadful news – so ghastly he'd not even told Herbert. Bessie Miller was to be betrothed! To Baron Godric de Mordon of the pendulous stomach – an elderly widower four times her age, with jowls like a bloodhound and hairs in his ears like the bristles on a Christmas hog.

Chapter 2

fiddler's Hill

The cold moonlight sparkled on the tears that flowed unchecked down Bessie Miller's cheeks as she crept into the great circle of standing stones on Fiddler's Hill, a leather pail in one hand, a storm lantern in the other and a sack slung loosely around her neck under her winter cloak. Her feet were wet but the numbness in her heart had seeped like icy water down through her limbs, so that she hardly felt the chill in her toes. She gazed desolately around the lonely pillars that rose from the icy scrub, looking for the column that the pedlar had described when he'd sold her the banishing spell at the Yuletide Fair.

It was not so foggy here as down in the valley of the River Twist, where the great mill wheel of her home at Tirley Grange lay trapped in the frozen river, and Bessie had no difficulty in picking out the single column of granite, set apart from the rest. The morning sun would rise behind it, and it was here that she stopped and set down her pail. She shivered. It was a barren, eerie place. It was said the great pillars were nine girls caught dancing with the devil on the Sabbath. He played his fiddle so fast they couldn't stop dancing and fell down dead. But Tom said it was a heathen temple, where the Druids had once worshipped the sun.

Kneeling down beside the pail, Bessie dragged at the cord around her neck, catching her breath impatiently as it snagged in her damp curls as she hurriedly looped the pouch over her head. She fumbled inside, pulled out an assortment of household items, and laid them cautiously on the snow in the shadow of the standing stone: one black candle, one wooden spoon, one silver mirror and a piece of folded parchment. She smoothed the crumpled spell against the damp fabric of her cloak. Then squinting at the parchment in the lamplight, she began to chant the banishing spell under her breath:

'Child of the moon, element of water
Reflect, distract, direction alter.
Goddess of Love, true may you prove
Banish *his face, by your good grace.*

'Now say his name three times,' she read, 'and light the black candle.' Bessie's heart was thumping but her hand was steady as she held the wick of the candle towards the lantern flame. 'Godric de Mordon,' she breathed softly. And then more strongly, 'Godric de Mordon . . . Baron Godric de Mordon.'

Then taking up the wooden spoon she dipped it into the pail and stirred the water three times clockwise and three times counter-clockwise to reverse bad luck, chanting as she stirred:

'Bright moon rising and shining above,
Shine down on this circle reveal my true love.'

Strangely excited, Bessie crossed the fingers of her left hand and stretched out her right to grasp the cold handle of the silver mirror.

'Bessie Miller!' Her mother's shrill voice sliced through the frosty air.

Bessie spun round with a scream of surprise and leapt to her feet, dropping the mirror.

'Bessie! In the name of heaven! What are you doing? Your soul will fly straight to hell!' Alice Miller snatched up her cloak as she ran, stumbling towards Bessie over the ragged ground. She stared in horror at the scattered objects on the grass, her hand to her mouth, and then, forming a hasty sign of the cross, she grabbed her daughter roughly by the shoulders. 'What would the priest say if he saw you? God forgive you, Bessie! This is witchcraft!'

Bessie squirmed in her mother's grasp, shaking herself free. 'Let go of me!' she cried. 'Let go!' She stumbled backwards, her black eyes blazing. 'How *could* you agree to it? He's revolting!' Bessie began to laugh, a high-pitched sound that was almost a cry. And then her tears began to flow. 'I never dreamed he would be so disgusting, even in my worst nightmares,' she sobbed. She bit her lip and squeezed her eyes tight shut. She couldn't forget the dinner at Micklow Manor, ancestral home of Sir Ranulf de Lacy, Lord of the Manor. Or the image of Baron Godric de Mordon – his flabby body, wobbling towards her over the tiled floor, bloodshot eyes flicking greedily over her. 'You must have seen his stomach!' she cried. 'Bursting out of his bright green hose, like a . . . like an overripe gooseberry!'

Bessie's mother shuddered inwardly but this was not the time for sympathy. Things had not been easy for her either. She had once been a de Lacy, daughter of Sir Ranulf himself, before they had become estranged and she had married a miller. But now Sir Ranulf had at last claimed kin and this was a chance for Bessie that might never come again. 'You must understand,' said Alice more gently. 'We're only trying to do our best for you. This is a far better match than a miller's daughter could ever dream of. We don't have money to buy you a husband and Baron Godric de Mordon is rich with fine lands and a manor. I'm grateful that Sir Ranulf has forgiven me, recognized you as his granddaughter and found you such a suitor . . .'

'Grateful!' exploded Bessie, her eyes wide with rage. 'I'm glad you're grateful! His head is bald and pimply like the skin of a plucked chicken!'

Alice bowed her head to hide the anguish in her eyes. She could feel Bessie's pain, but the family had need of this match. There'd been precious little work for her husband, Gabriel, since the summer just gone – and money was as scarce as snowflakes in summer.

'Be sensible, Bessie, please,' reasoned her mother. 'You can't marry a villein or a serf. Not when I was born a de Lacy. And yet you're not exactly gentry are you? Your father is the best of men but he's still only a miller.' An arrow of strain creased her brow. 'I'm truly sorry, Bessie. I wish it were not like this but sometimes we just have to do the best we can.' She squeezed Bessie's shoulder, forcing a smile. 'There'll be a fine dowry,' she said more brightly. 'Your grandfather has been most generous: a feather bed, full ninety marks, six silver spoons . . .'

'Silver spoons!' spat Bessie. 'Is that what I'm worth now? Six silver spoons! Oh, and a feather bed. Let's not forget the bed!'

Alice pulled her cloak more tightly about her thin frame. 'That's enough now, Bessie,' she said, a new determination in her voice. 'You're a will o' the wisp with your head full of dreams. But dreams are not real life. You're a woman now. And besides,' she said firmly, 'it is decided. So you will return to Tirley Grange with me now. Tomorrow is Christmas Eve and you will accompany Baron Godric de Mordon to Saint Wilfred's Abbey to watch the Christmas play.' She glanced warily at the leather pail, the wooden spoon and the stub of black candle lying in the frozen grass. 'And there must be no more of this dangerous nonsense,' she said, lowering her voice, although they were quite alone in the stone circle. 'Folk will say you're a pagan, and then where will you be?'

Chapter 3

Tracks in the Snow

As Bessie Miller was lighting the black candle up on Fiddler's Hill, Tom Fletcher was hurrying after Abbot Fergus, two bulging saddlebags slung around his neck.

'Will ye nae stop prattling, young Tom?' complained Abbot Fergus wearily in his soft Scottish burr as he shouldered open the door of his new study in the abbot's house, his shaggy lurcher, Mungo, yelping a welcome at his heels. The abbot was pleased to see Tom, his favourite novice, but he was also wet and tired, exhausted from two hard days on the road from London. 'And you're treading on my travelling cloak! God's teeth, were ye lying in wait for me?'

The abbot was right. Tom and the dog had been lurking by the west gate of the abbey for most of the evening, peering down the high-hedged track, ears like hares for the sound of hooves in the snow.

'But Brother Fergus . . . I . . . I mean to say . . . *Abbot* . . . I must talk to you before it's too late!' pleaded Tom. 'I simply can't take my vows. I'm not ready . . .'

The abbot pulled his grizzled beard. '*Abbot* Fergus, indeed!' he laughed, avoiding Tom's eyes. 'Now who would have thought it? My new title will take a wee while to get used to . . . along with these new rooms.' He raised a fiery eyebrow, taking in the jug of spiced wine and roast woodcock placed ready on a trestle by the fire. 'Put the bags by the hearth, there's a good fellow,' he said briskly, 'and run along to vespers. I can hear the hand bell ringing.'

'But Abbot Fergus,' wailed Tom. 'You're not even listening . . .'

The abbot clicked his tongue, and heaving a weary sigh, placed his large hands on Tom's shoulders. 'By heaven, you've grown even more – and I've only been gone a few days!' He passed an anxious hand through the stormy red hair that curled crisply around his tonsure. 'Now listen to me, Tom. There can be no more talk of avoiding your vows. Ye will have heard the expression "beggars can't be choosers". Well you're not a chooser – few novices are. But you're not a beggar either, nor will ye be so long as you're here in Saint Wilfred's. And I can tell ye, I've seen my share of beggars these last few days in London and it's nae a pretty sight. Ye should know when you're well off Tom and thank God there's a Yuletide table laid for ye here.'

Tom stared miserably at his boots. 'Aye, ye'd do well to look at your good sturdy boots,' sighed the abbot. 'I tell ye, I've seen feet black with frostbite in London. The city's a fearful place – grubby alleys full of cut-purses, thieves and beggars. And the taverns, now: gamblers, tricksters, all manner of evil lurking there.' Abbot Fergus gazed sadly at Tom. 'I'm sorry, Brother Tom, but there really is no way out. The bishop has made up his mind. We have too many novices of a certain age, and you're chief novice remember – the eldest of all. So I'm afraid we have to make you all into real monks on Christmas Day. No exceptions made, Tom, not even for you.'

Abbot Fergus shook his head sorrowfully as the door clicked shut. He felt for Brother Thomas but there really was no other choice for these penniless boys. He shivered. The study was as cold as death in spite of the fire, yet he was grateful for the freeze. In winter the roads could run like rivers of mud and he'd been anxious to get home – and not only because of the snow.

He moved heavily over to the fire, breathing in the comforting smell of Mungo, who was warming his back by the hearthside. Crouching down, he spread out his fingers to the blaze, then puffed out his cheeks and glanced nervously at his damp saddlebags. The abbot hesitated, and then with a fleeting look over his shoulder, he stretched out his hand towards the bulging leather bag . . . then swiftly pulled it back. He scrambled to his feet and hurried anxiously to the casement, snatched open the lattice shutter and peeped suspiciously out. *Of course there was no-one there! How silly of him!* The snow was smooth, glistening in the lights that spilled from the abbey windows. He frowned, annoyed at his own foolishness, and yet his heart was thumping. Glancing warily at the saddlebag, he strode over to the door and turned the key. Then, stealing like a thief to the fireside, he unfastened the leather thongs and pulled a small object from inside.

It was a pouch of greenish-brown skin with a curious lumpy texture, unlike any leather he had ever seen before. And inside the bag, wrapped in a soft damask cloth, was a golden casket inlaid with silver flames which glowed with a light of their own. The hairs rose on the back of his neck. It was the most exquisite thing he had ever seen, so why the churning in his stomach – a kind of fluttering that almost felt like fear?

Abbot Fergus sighed. Perhaps he had been a fool to agree to take the casket without asking more questions. But the sacrist of Westminster Abbey had been so persuasive, so desperate to urge it upon him as he was fastening his riding cloak in readiness to depart from London yesterday morning. It wasn't even as if he liked the sacrist of Westminster Abbey. In truth he found Brother Gideon rather repellent, but it had seemed a small favour at the time and why should he refuse?

'*It is only for a little while, I beg you,*' Brother Gideon had pleaded, pressing the bag into his hands. The plump sacrist had been sweating although the water clock dripped diamonds of ice. '*Just a safe place until it can be returned to London,*' he had whispered in Fergus's ear. '*There is no risk for you, I promise. I cannot explain to you now. But I will come to your abbey soon and retrieve the casket myself.*'

And so Abbot Fergus had agreed. He had the kindest of hearts and after all, the fat monk was a fellow sacrist, and Abbot Fergus had ample room for the small chest in his saddlebags along with his old robes. Yet from the first, almost before he had trotted beneath the narrow arch of the eastern gate of the city to leave the squalor of London behind him, he had been filled with a strange unease. A curious sensation had dogged every icy rut between the twisted alleys of London and the coastal town of Saint Agnes Next-the-Sea. Abbot Fergus had felt sure he was being followed.

The voices of the novices fluting from the chapel broke into his reverie as he knelt in the rushes by the fire. The abbot jumped to his feet and strode quickly to the window, this time flinging wide the shutters and staring out across the snow-filled water meadow leading down to the River Twist. There was not a soul in sight, not even a winter owl, but now there were unmistakeable tracks that had not been there before. Fresh marks in the snow, cutting a path across the water meadow, the heel towards the river and the toe pointing straight in the direction of the abbot's study window.

Abbot Fergus wasn't the worrying kind. And yet his hand trembled as he turned from the window and poured himself a large goblet of spicy wine and drank it to the dregs in one swift gulp. The fiery liquid coursed through his veins with a shiver of warmth. He sank down in a cushioned chair and began to unlace his boots. *There must be some simple explanation for the tracks. A novice on the run from vespers perhaps, or a beggar seeking shelter for the night in the warmth of the abbey wall.* He poured himself another goblet of wine, leaned back in his chair and closed his eyes. He must be imagining things. All this travelling had exhausted his mind. *A good night's sleep and these fancies will melt away.*

And with that comforting thought his head began to nod. For Abbot Fergus could never have guessed that around the casket there had once been a pure white cord, three knots along its length, ending with a moonstone in the shape of a tear. Nor could he possibly have known that Brother Gideon of Westminster Abbey lay dead, freshly pulled from the River Thames and cold as a fish on market day, a horizontal weal across his neck that gleamed blue-black in the flickering light of a humble watchman's lantern.

Chapter 4

A Flash of Silver

A fringe of icicles hung from the snow-laden thatch of *The Frisky Friar Inn*, but inside the low-beamed parlour it was a merry fug of warmth and torchlight, the thick sacking on the windows keeping the east wind out and the raucous laughter in. A fire of brushwood was heaped in the wide hearth, a brace of wood pigeons revolving slowly on an iron spit. The tavern had been a popular meeting place for the monks from Saint Wilfred's Abbey for many a long year. However there were no monks here on the night before Christmas Eve. Only a ragged assortment of locals playing backgammon, or telling a fortune or two with the stones. No one of any importance, unless you counted a stranger in a dark travelling cloak, who sat in a shadowy corner, his amber eyes turned from the firelight and his hood pulled over his head. His tankard of ale lay untouched before him and he was listening intently to the careless talk at the tables.

'No Brother Ethelwig, tonight?' said the landlord's wife to Job Pug, Ethelwig's faithful servant.

'Not tonight, Beatrice,' replied old Job, tearing a hunk of bread from a crusty loaf on the hearth. 'Abbot Fergus is newly arrived from London so the monks are busy at the abbey. I'd be ringing out the bells in welcome if them stonemasons had got a move on with the new tower. It will be spring at least afore it's finished.'

'So no more flying for Brother Ethelwig this year, I reckon,' she laughed. 'Poor soul! I hear his new flying machine's almost finished. He'll just have to be patient for a while.'

'Don't you worry about him,' smiled Job. 'He's keeping himself out of mischief. A fire-breathing bird for the Christmas feast! That's the latest.'

Beatrice rolled her eyes, spinning round as an icy wind sliced in from the newly open door, raising the skirts of her kirtle. Two men had entered the smoky tavern, thrusting the sackcloth aside in a flurry of snow that settled in their travelling hoods like swans' down. Everyone looked towards the door, including the silent stranger.

The landlord bustled eagerly to greet the newcomers, his hands held out in welcome. Business was none too brisk in winter and he was grateful for any passing trade. But the visitors shrank back behind the sackcloth, drawing him out into the yard. So it was only the hospitable landlord who noticed the flame-shaped mark in the centre of their foreheads . . . and their almond eyes as black as sloe berries.

* * *

The landlord huddled his cloak around him as he lit the way across the cobbles towards the sleeping barn, holding his lantern high.

'What brings you to *The Frisky Friar* on a wild night like this?' he asked the visitors in a friendly voice, fumbling with the key in the frozen lock. 'Not that it's any business of mine,' he added with an apologetic cough into the frosty silence. He shouldered the iron-studded door and hung the lantern on a hook screwed to a smoke-blackened beam. 'Our barn is warm and dry enough and you can have any hay pallet you choose,' he went on. 'You'd not recognize this barn in summer. Crammed to the rafters with pilgrims come to see Saint Wilfred's bunion. But you've only a hog for company this evening. Would a penny a night sound fair?'

The dark-skinned strangers inclined their heads with a formality that reminded the landlord of summer traders from the east. Then the taller of the two slipped his hand into his robe and pulled out a pouch of crimson silk, offering it to the landlord with a deep low bow. The bald little man peered into the pouch and then his eyes grew round as plum puddings. He blinked and peered again. The light was dim – only a guttering lantern – but nestling in the bag were five precious stones: sea green and purple, scarlet, turquoise and blue.

The astonished landlord scurried back across the cobbles a grin of delight on his honest round face. He couldn't believe his luck. He burst in through the door, catching his plump wife around her comfortable waist and spinning her round, dangling the purse in front of her nose.

'Put me down, husband!' she giggled, flushing with pleasure. 'Anyone would think it was Christmas Eve already!' She sniffed, wrinkling her nose. 'Take that thing away,' she laughed. 'It smells like them sour yellow things they bring in on the ships in summer.'

Over in the shadowy corner beyond the reach of the firelight, the hooded stranger was preparing to leave. He beckoned to the landlord who scurried across the room. The man selected a silver penny from his purse, printed with the sign of the cross. Bustling to the wall, the landlord took down a pair of iron coin-shears from a hook and cut the coin into four equal parts, returning three to the traveller's open palm. A splinter of light glinted from the stranger's hand. The landlord frowned. Three of his fingers were flesh and blood but the fourth was hard and cold and flashed in the light as if it were made of silver.

Chapter 5

The Honey Jar

Tom Fletcher lay on his hay pallet, listening to the scratching of the frosty twigs on the shutters and the gentle breathing of the other novices in the dormitory. He rolled over for the hundredth time, then turned onto his back and gazed in despair at the flames of the oil lamps, dancing on the midnight ceiling. His skin itched and he felt hot even though there had been ice on the water bucket before he went to bed.

Flinging back the stifling blankets, he thrust his hand under his bolster and pulled out Bessie's letter. Then, with a furtive glance along the rows of sleeping boys, he padded across the rushes to the window and stared down into the cloisters. The moon hung amongst the scaffolding of the half-finished tower, so it was light enough for him to read the hurriedly scribbled words that he'd read twenty times already since the servant had slipped the note into his lap at dinner.

Tom,

I've made up my mind. I would rather die than marry that odious old man! I know where I can find a little money, enough perhaps to take me to London. Come with me, Tom! Don't let them trap you too. If you want to join me, then meet me tomorrow after the novices' play – at the east end of the abbey under the rose window. I don't expect you have money but bring whatever you can lay hands on. Please come! This might be our only chance to get away!

Bessie

Tom leaned his head against the cold stone pillar that divided the dormitory window in two, a knot of panic in his stomach. A vision of Bessie floated into his mind in a swirl of black curls. *How can I run away to London? I haven't a penny*, he fretted. He stroked the stubble on his top lip with a frown. *But then I can't let her go on her own. There might be thieves or wolves . . .* He groaned in frustration. *He couldn't*, wouldn't *take his vows! Abbot Fergus was wrong. This might be a good life for some . . . but not for Tom Fletcher!* Over on his pallet, Herbert grunted and laughed gently in his sleep. Tom gazed sadly at his friend. *But then again, how can I explain to Herbert . . .*

He turned back to the window, but this time his attention was distracted by a light in the sacristy – a small bobbing point like a candle flame where he was sure there'd been darkness before. *Odd*, thought Tom with a glance at the water clock. *It must be an hour until matins so who could be up at this time?* He lifted a cresset lamp from the end of his sleeping pallet. There was no harm in taking a look. So, hastily pushing Bessie's note back under his bolster, he crept softly in the direction of the night stairs that lead straight from the dormitory into the nave of the church.

Bessie Miller stared anxiously out of the window of her garret room at Tirley Grange Mill over the rows of winter vegetables. She chafed her hands, where the frozen leaves had ripped her fingers as she'd pulled turnips from the icy ground that morning. *'Just think, Bessie,'* her mother had said with a nervous laugh, *'you'll have servants to pick turnips when you're Lady de Mordon.'*

Bessie pushed herself away from the window with a groan, catching sight of her reflection in the looking glass as she turned. A wild-haired gypsy gazed defiantly back, her head haloed by stars. 'We'll see about Baron de Mordon,' she whispered fiercely. 'Come on, Bessie,' she breathed, blinking back tears of rage, 'you can't let this happen to you. It's time for action!'

Turning from the mirror, she lit an oil lamp from a candle, trimming the wick so it burned firm and bright. And then she crept stealthily from her room, tiptoed across the landing and down the stairs, avoiding the creaking step with an expert hop and entered the freezing kitchen. The familiar pots and pans cast shadows in the gloom and her mother's old workbasket, its coloured silks spilling onto the cold stone hearth, brought a lump to her throat. She paused, feeling her resolve beginning to slip away and then she shook her head angrily. *They should feel guilty, not me!*

Kneeling down, she prised up a loose stone and silently slid the cupboard key from its hiding place. She glanced warily over her shoulder as she crept towards the cabinet. 'They've left me no choice,' she muttered, cringing at the click of the lock. Her heart skipped a beat. She'd confided her plans in nobody except Tom. Not even her best friend Abigail Abrahams. Abbi was too sensible. Too down to earth by far. But more importantly, Abbi couldn't tell a lie. And Bessie couldn't take the chance of telling her friend, however deceitful that made her feel.

The honey jar clinked with promise as she lifted it down. Bessie held her breath as her cold fingers fumbled in the pot . . . and then relief flooded in like warm summer wine. It must be half full of silver pennies – enough for a passage to London.

It was clammy and damp in the church and Tom's teeth chattered as he scurried across the stone-flagged floor towards the sacristy passage. The cold seeped through the soles of his night-slippers, turning his knees to ice. Perhaps he should have stayed in bed under his rabbit-skin blanket. He stopped outside the sacristy door. There was definitely a light. *Who could be there at this hour?*

Tom lifted the latch and peered in. The stout monk's back was turned but he would have recognized those plump legs anywhere, the too-short habit revealing calves glowing white in the darkness. The only light was a shaft of moonlight from a circular window set in the wall at the back. *Or was that all . . .* For on the table lay the strangest golden casket set with tiny silver flames, which seemed to shine with a strange radiance. Tom's breath caught in his throat.

The abbot started at the sound, spinning round with a cry. He sprang towards Tom, grabbed him by the wrist and twisted it hard. Tom's oil lamp flared as he jumped back, illuminating the angry face of Abbot Fergus. 'How dare you come in here?' roared the abbot.

'It's . . . it's only me,' stammered Tom, shocked at his furious tone. 'I saw a light in the sacristy . . . I . . . I couldn't sleep . . . I thought there might be an intruder . . .' Shakily, he placed the oil lamp on the edge of the table and began to massage his wrist where the abbot had pinched his skin.

Abbot Fergus moved swiftly for a bulky man, placing his body in front of the casket on the table. 'What did you see?' he demanded.

Tom realised he was trembling – but not with cold. *What was going on? The face hardly looked like the abbot he knew at all, the expression so sinister and strange.* 'I . . . I saw a little chest . . . a beautiful golden casket . . .' he said unsteadily. 'Did you bring it from London?'

Abbot Fergus took a step towards Tom, his face softening for a moment. 'It is a mere trinket that I am . . . ahem . . . looking after for the sacrist of Westminster Abbey.' And then his face hardened again. 'Tell no one of this. If you breathe so much as a word of what you have seen to any one, I will have you flung into the abbey dungeon, as God is my witness!'

Tom needed no second bidding. He turned on his heel and ran. Forgetting his oil lamp, he fled, blind as a mole down the sacristy passage, grazing his hands on the dank stone walls and up the night-stairs to the dormitory. Flinging himself down on his pallet he pulled his fur blanket up over his head. His heart was pumping like a peddler's drum. He was mystified. *What could be wrong with Fergus?* Tom's knuckles were bleeding but he hardly felt the pain. He was shocked to the core. There'd been something deeply alarming in the abbot's face as he'd turned from the casket; a look of greedy hunger before his face flared into anger. '*Just a trinket,*' Abbot Fergus had said.

Tom didn't believe him.

Chapter 6

The Garland Spell

The following day was set fair for a perfect Christmas Eve. The recent fog had cleared and the grass sparkled white in the thin sunshine. There was enough snow for snowballing and a quiver of expectation hung in the sharp air as the novices scurried about the abbey with arms full of gaudy costumes for the entertainment. The novices' play was a tradition at Saint Wilfred's and nobody in Saint Agnes would miss it for all the herrings in a winter barrel. Monks with brooms and shovels cleared snow from the outer court to make way for the abbey carpenter and his apple-cheeked apprentice who hauled and shoved the great two-tiered stage into position on its rickety wheels and began to dust it free of a year's supply of cobwebs.

Everyone was excited. Everyone that is, except Tom, who struggled through the day, his mind in turmoil, one minute hopeful, his head full of daring schemes to flee to London, the next anxious and fretful, filled with a numb sense of inevitability – of the permanent change in his life that Christmas Day would bring. And there was something else too. A nagging feeling of foreboding, like snakes in the pit of his stomach . . . and he just couldn't shake it off. That midnight meeting with Abbot Fergus had really unnerved him. What could the abbot's strange behaviour really mean?

At last it was early evening, and the novices were gathered in the tithe barn of the abbey. Some were struggling into their costumes for the play whilst others, up to their elbows in leather buckets, were staining their arms brown with walnut juice.

'Look, my husband, behold an inn! Pray knock on the door that we may come in,' recited Brother Felix from deep inside the blue hood of the Virgin Mary's robe.

'Alas, there is no room,' replied Odo, dressed as a carpenter with an iron saw at his waist.

Tom glared at Odo. The chief novice always played Joseph, so why had Brother Dunstan given Tom the part of a donkey? He thumped a hay bale with the hoof of his costume. He was in no mood for a Christmas play and to make matters worse, Ed, the youngest novice, was prattling incessantly in his ear. Some nonsense about dusky strangers in the stable with eyes as black as ravens' wings!

'It's the truth!' insisted Edmund. 'They were hiding in the hay loft. Come and see if you don't believe me!'

'It must have been the brown boggart!' said Tom sarcastically. He loomed over Edmund, his eyes goggling. 'Its eyes are balls of fire and its breath stinks worse than Brother Dunstan's!'

Ed shrank away in terror, tumbling backwards over a bale of spiky hay.

'Don't tease him,' snapped Herbert, hauling Ed to his feet and adjusting the corn halo on his curls. He was fed up with Tom, jumpy and nervous one minute and poking fun the next. 'You know that story scares him.'

'Ed needs to learn to take a joke,' said Tom harshly, 'and stop making things up!' He picked up a sack stuffed with hay, two holes cut for eyes and a ragged pair of ears on the top, and pulled it over his head.

'But I'm not making it up!' wailed Ed. 'I really did see them . . . two brown-skinned monks hiding in the stables. Their eyes were black and they had curved noses like eagles' beaks.' He paused. 'At least they were dressed like monks,' he added uncertainly, 'but they're not from *this* abbey!'

Herbert was watching Ed closely. 'I'm going to go and have a look for myself, Tom,' he said coldly. '*Before* I accuse Ed of lying.'

Tom lifted the donkey's head from his shoulders. 'You can waste your time if you like, Herbert,' he said turning his back. 'But I'm going to see what's happening in the outer court. I'll only be a minute.'

Sheep's feet were Tom's favourite, sticky on the outside and juicy in the middle. There were pig's liver rissoles too on the festive stalls in the outer court where the townspeople were gathering. Hot meat crackled and jumped in the flat iron pans. Tom felt better now. As dusk had fallen he'd finally made up his mind that he would go with Bessie. He didn't have any money but at least he could pinch some food for the journey. His eyes combed the little knots of people in the smoky lantern light, searching for Bessie in vain amidst the stalls selling spiced wine and holiday trinkets. *It's all in a good cause*, he told himself as he slunk round the back of the butcher's barrow, his donkey head clutched in his hand. *It's not exactly stealing*.

'Merry Christmas Eve, Mistress Pug,' cried the sweaty faced butcher as he cranked the handle of a glowing spit, spiked like an edible necklace with stuffed blackbirds and thrushes. 'What can I do for you? You'd best fill your belly. After this it'll be nothing but salted herring through 'till spring!'

'I'll take a roasted blackbird if you please, John,' laughed Mistress Pug, shifting baby Amos on her thin hip. 'And one of them crusty rolls.' Her youngest child looked hot and uncomfortable, swaddled tight under countless layers of cloth. In his role as the baby Jesus, he'd have to lie in the manger for quite some time and Mistress Pug wasn't taking any chances.

From his hiding place behind the barrow, Tom watched her move off, her face ruddy in the lantern light. The butcher turned and reached for one of his knives and whilst his broad back was turned, Tom took his chance. Crouching low at the side of the stall, he shot out a hand and grabbed one crusty roll and then another, stuffing them down the front of his donkey costume as he ducked swiftly back behind the booth into the shadows. His mouth was watering. The roast blackbirds smelled delicious but they'd be far too greasy to stuff down his robe! He tightened his belt to secure the stolen goods, then ran at a crouch behind the stalls, shrinking into the shadows like a cat who had stolen the dinner, emerging into the open when he thought the coast was clear – straight into the path of Brother Ambrose, the quill master.

'I'm . . . I'm sorry Brother Ambrose,' blurted Tom, a rush of blood to his cheeks. He felt as if the quill master could see right through his clothes to the warm rolls nestling above his belt.

Brother Ambrose stared at him oddly. 'Is everything all right, Tom? You look hot and bothered. Ready for your vows tomorrow?'

Tom backed away. 'Y-yes. I . . . I feel as if I'm just about ready!'

'I've made you a new quill in honour of the occasion,' said the quill master with a merry crease of his eyes. 'It's the flight feather of a Barn Owl . . .'

Sir Ranulf de Lacy's cart rumbled under the arch of the west gate of Saint Wilfred's bouncing over the uneven cobbles. Bessie had wanted to walk but her grandfather insisted they ride in his wagon. She glared with loathing at the stout form of Baron Godric de Mordon, wobbling along on the high seat in front, next to Sir Ranulf, his fat buttocks spilling over the wooden seat. Bessie's heart fluttered with anxiety. Thank heavens Abbi wouldn't be here asking awkward questions. As a Jew she always stayed away from the Christmas play, and for once Bessie felt relieved that her friend wouldn't be with her.

It was uncomfortably hot under three layers of scratchy

woollen shifts, two skirts and a squirrel-lined cloak, yet she dared not fidget in case her mother heard the clinking of the money in her purse. Bessie touched the charm ribbon around her neck – holly berries for faithfulness, junipers to protect her pledge and creamy mistletoe to complete the garland spell. She could hardly bear the tension. *Would Tom come with her or not?*

'By the water in my blood,' she murmured, fingering the berries like a rosary, 'By the rivers of the earth,

By the tides of the moon,

Bring me one who knows my worth.'

Chapter 7

A Dark and Dangerous Web

The stage wagon had been positioned between two yew trees at Brother Ethelwig's request. He'd been very secretive about his latest invention and there was much speculation about the tangle of ropes and pulleys draped between the topmost branches of the trees. But all was revealed at last. Ethelwig, perched precariously on the highest of rickety ladders had finally attached the enormous straw star in position. His stomach bubbled with excitement. The black powder was in place. He'd measured it out carefully – just enough for the star to fizz across the stage with a tail of sparks, leading the shepherds to the manger. Too little and it would fizzle out ahead of time, too much and it would whizz like a firecracker – and that would spoil the effect.

The play was about to begin and baby Amos Pug was screaming lustily from the manger. Bessie sat beside the Baron on the front row of rough benches arranged before the stage, an honour reserved for Sir Ranulf de Lacy, the Lord of the Manor, and his party. Fustian, Sir Ranulf's clerk, perched on the bench behind. The baron squeezed Bessie's hand.

'Quite comfortable, my dear?' he said in a blast of onion breath. Fustian stared at the baron's fat neck. *What was Sir Ranulf thinking of, betrothing his lovely granddaughter to this coarse old mountain of blubber?* But then again, Fustian knew refinement wasn't everything. Sir Percy FitzNigel, his previous master, might have had perfect manners, but his heart was as cruel as a crow.

Bessie, however, was pleased to be sitting at the front, even if it did mean sitting next to the lecherous baron. She peered hard at the stage. She couldn't see Tom anywhere. The chief novice always took the part of Joseph and yet it certainly wasn't Tom sitting by the manger with the Virgin Mary. Joseph's face was stained with walnut juice but there was no mistaking Odo's pompous expression. So where in the world was Tom?

Bessie had almost given up hope when suddenly her eyes were drawn to the donkey standing behind the manger. It seemed to be wagging its head in her direction. She leaned forward in her seat and the donkey leaned forward too and as it did, it raised a hoof. Bessie raised her hand and let it drop. The donkey dropped its hoof too. She nodded her head up and down. The donkey nodded in reply.

In the cool sacristy at the east end of the abbey church, Abbot Fergus touched the golden casket with his finger. He really should hurry. He was already late for the novices' play. He could hear the drums and bagpipes from across the cloisters. He picked up the golden chest and cradled it in his arm. Why did it have this strange power over him? He should lock it away now, but there was something about it, something that drew him back to the locked sacristy cupboard almost every hour – just to have another peep. He started violently and rushed to the door, staring nervously up and down the passage outside. He was sure he'd heard a scuffling sound . . . but of course there was nobody there. It was Christmas Eve after all and everyone was waiting for him in the outer court.

But the abbot needn't have worried. In the bustle and excitement, no-one had noticed that Abbot Fergus was missing and the play had already begun. Sir Ranulf de Lacy assumed he was sitting with the monks, and the monks that their abbot had joined the Lord of the Manor's party. So there was nobody looking for him at all; no-one around to hear his startled cry. In fact the abbot himself had scarcely heard the slow footfall behind him. The hairs on the back of his neck had only just started to rise when he felt himself seized from behind. The arm that snaked around his neck was mahogany brown in colour, and in the hair's breadth of a second before he fell helpless to the ground, the abbot noticed an exotic smell. That same curious aroma that had dogged his every step from the city of Westminster on the great bow bend of the River Thames to Saint Wilfred's Abbey on the peaceful tributary of the Twist.

Meanwhile, in Saint Wilfred's courtyard, the shepherds had gathered by the side of the stage, gazing anxiously up into the branches of the yew tree for the signal from Ethelwig.

'Ready down below?' he called at last. The shepherds hitched their robes and began to scramble onto the stage.

'The shepherds heard the story,' they chanted tunefully,

'Proclaimed by angels bright

How Christ the Lord of Glory

Was born on earth this night.'

There was a hissing sound like a hundred serpents and a shower of sparks flew glittering into the trees. The ropes across the stage vibrated with a dull hum and the straw star began to move, shakily at first and then gathering speed, faster and faster it whooshed across the stage, scarlet flames streaming out behind like a comet's tail. There was a flurry of applause, *oohs* and *aahs* of wonder, then all of a sudden, with a monstrous bang, the huge star turned a somersault and exploded into flames, lurching and spitting in the force of the blast until it came to a juddering halt, directly above the manger. Mary and Joseph leapt from the stage followed by a tumble of assorted sheep and oxen. The donkey shrieked and lunged for the manger, tearing baby Amos from the crib – and just in time! For a second later and the smouldering star came plummeting down, landing with a fizz in the middle of the straw.

'Water!'

'A bucket!'

'A blanket!'

Now the manger was on fire and the hay bales behind had also caught light. As the audience ran like frightened rabbits, Tom saw his chance. He thrust the howling baby into Mistress Pug's arms and raced across the outer court towards the dairy, elbowing his way through the crush of bodies without a backward glance. Thick smoke billowed from the burning stage. Tom could hardly believe his luck. Skirting the stables, he skidded on the slippery grass, around the back of the kennels, the laundry and the brew house. He paused to glance over his shoulder, praying no-one was hurt, then ran like a hare in the shadow of the great nave of the abbey until he reached the pile of rubble and scaffolding at the base of the bell tower. Rounding the corner, he flung off the donkey's head and leant coughing against the stone buttress at the east end of the abbey. Just where Bessie had said. Directly under the rose window and less than twenty paces from the sacristy.

Panting, he squinted into the darkness, smoke stinging his throat. He could see the river, curling away east in moonlight and shadow. The hubbub from the outer court was silenced now by the enormous bulk of the abbey that reared above him like a mountain. The cry of an owl made him start. Alone in the shadow of the tower, the night seemed full of threatening shapes and otherworldly sounds. And then, quite plainly, he heard a dull thud followed by a sound that was distinctly of this world; the splintering noise of breaking glass.

Bessie too had grabbed her chance. She walked quickly across the cobbles, her hood pulled over her face. She didn't want to run for fear of attracting attention. Away from the outer court the lights were fewer, and deep in the shadow of the north face of the abbey, she picked up her skirts and ran awkwardly, the joy of escape mingled with a hollow feeling of fear. She'd convinced herself she would run away, even if Tom wouldn't join her. But now she realised she'd been fooling herself. *What if Tom had changed his mind?*

Her heart thudding in her throat, Bessie crept around the huge stone buttresses at the base of the tower. She stifled a cry of relief. There was Tom, crouching in the shadows. She started towards him but something in his manner made her stop. 'Shhh!' he hissed, pointing up at the sacristy window.

Bessie shrank into the shadow of the abbey wall. A hooded form crouched on the wide sill, clinging to the stone gargoyles. And then the shape leapt, agile as a cat, landing with a crunch on the broken glass below. With a furtive glance over its shoulder, the figure peered back up at the window. A small dark object plummeted down, caught deftly in the intruder's outstretched hands. And then another hooded shape appeared and with equal agility climbed down the wall, feet sure as a goat in the footholds of the sandstone walls.

'They look like monks!' breathed Bessie.

'They're not our monks. Thieves more like. This is the sacristy. It's full of the abbey treasure!'

Suddenly Abbot Fergus's face swam into Tom's mind; that curious expression of greed and longing as he had gazed at the golden casket. *The golden casket! The one that Abbot Fergus had brought from London!* There was no time to explain to Bessie. The two figures were making off, racing across the moonlit snowfield leading to the eastern gate.

'Quick, let's follow them,' whispered Tom, grabbing Bessie's hand. 'We can't let them get away!'

Bessie snatched it back. 'But what about our plan?' she said indignantly. 'I thought we were going to London!'

'There'll be time for that later. Come on! We must go after them!' Tom broke into a run. 'Thank heavens for the snow. We can follow their tracks.'

'Wait, Tom!' hissed Bessie, stamping her foot, but Tom had already set off. There was no stopping him in this mood. So Bessie picked up her skirts and began to follow, keeping the snow tracks in view.

Tom gave no thought to what they might do if they caught up with the strangers. Tears of cold stung his eyes. Plans for escape would have to wait. All he knew for certain was that he had to follow the casket. If he stopped to fetch Abbot Fergus now, he'd lose sight of it forever.

For how was Tom to know that Abbot Fergus lay bleeding on the other side of the sacristy wall, sprawled under a pillar with a gash in his head, the blood still warm as it pooled on the cold stone floor? Nor could he ever have guessed at the threads of intrigue that joined the winding alleys of the city of London to the small coastal town of Saint Agnes Next-the-Sea. The strands were pulling together now, slowly but inexorably, and Bessie and Tom were being drawn into a dark and dangerous web.

Chapter 8

Los Tres Magos

Out in the wooded countryside the wind was razor sharp. Bessie and Tom followed the tracks, listening for a fall of snow up ahead to indicate a change of direction as the fugitives fled swiftly through the trees. They could hear the swollen river, plunging beside the track as it wove in and out of the ancient forest. By now the trees were thinning fast. It would be harder to remain unobserved in the scrubland and stubble fields between the forest and the harbour – the direction in which the thieves seemed to be heading.

It was snowing again, fat grey flakes settling thickly on their clothes and blurring their vision as Bessie and Tom darted between stunted bushes. They lost their quarry for an anxious few minutes in the swirling blizzard only to pick up the trail of the scurrying forms as they reached the outskirts of the town where a cluster of the poorest hovels crouched together for warmth. Down into the town they padded, using the ditches that bordered the side of the road for cover, over the stone bridge beside the churchyard and past the darkened windows of *The Frisky Friar*. Almost everyone not frail or sick was up at the abbey tonight. At the corner of Butcher Street, Bessie and Tom stopped in the darkness of a lean-to pigsty to catch their breath.

'This is madness, Tom!' panted Bessie, clutching his arm. 'Let's go back. What will we do when we catch up with them anyway? You seem to have completely forgotten our plan for London!'

Tom shook her hand off roughly. 'There's no time to explain. Trust me. I haven't forgotten – but this is something I have to do.'

So scurrying from one doorway to the next they pressed on again through the tangle of streets leading down to the quay.

The fishing boats tied up along the harbour wall were deserted, riding high in the water, black waves splashing against their bows. It had stopped snowing now and there was an intermittent moon. In the half-light Bessie and Tom could see the bulky shape of a larger craft, a glimmer of lantern light burning bleakly on deck. It was a smallish sea-going cog, the kind of trading vessel that could ply the North Sea with a small crew in all weathers. A dark figure stood on the deck beating his hands on his arms and stamping up and down beneath the mast. Every few paces he stopped and stared out across the harbour as if he was waiting for someone. He wore a sealskin cape and a fur cap, ear flaps pulled down against the piercing cold. As soon as he noticed the figures of the fugitives on the jetty, he uncoiled a rope ladder that dropped with a heavy thud. The two men hitched up their cloaks and climbed nimbly up the rungs, then dropped, silent as spiders, down onto the deck. The moon passed behind a cloud. Tom took his chance to dart across the wharf and behind a wooden smoke-house, dragging Bessie reluctantly by the hand.

'For heaven's sake, Tom! Stop!' gasped Bessie. 'We can't follow them on to the ship! Let's think this through.'

'Listen, Bessie,' whispered Tom. 'I'm almost certain I know what they took from the sacristy.' He hesitated, remembering his promise of secrecy to the abbot. But then again, he owed it to Bessie to tell her what he was dragging her into. 'If I'm right, it's not just any old bit of treasure. It's hard to explain but it's a golden casket Abbot Fergus brought from London. He's very . . . *attached* to it,' he said, searching for the word to describe the curious effect of the casket. 'I've never seen anything quite like it. But I know it's something I've got to get back for him!'

Tom rose from a crouch and peered cautiously around the corner. He guessed the seaman in the fur cap was the skipper. Whoever he was, he'd wasted no time in taking the men below, not even bothering to haul up the ladder, and now the deck looked deserted. 'Please come with me, Bessie,' begged Tom. 'If you don't I'll have to go alone. I can't let them get away with it.'

Bessie glared at Tom. They'd had battles of will before – both being as stubborn as each other. But Bessie knew Tom. And once he'd made up his mind, there was no stopping him. She peered sulkily over his shoulder but she knew in her heart that she'd follow him. '*Los Tres Magos*,' she whispered under her breath. The painted name on the stern of the ship gleamed white in the reflected light from the water.

'Do you recognize the name?'

Bessie shrugged. 'Never heard of it in my life,' she said less sullenly, 'but if we're going to climb that rope ladder, I need to get rid of one of these skirts!'

Chapter 9

The Man with the Silver Finger

lmost as soon as Bessie and Tom had dropped down on deck they heard the creak of feet ascending a wooden ladder. Someone was coming back up! They had little choice for a hideaway but they managed to squeeze behind a great pile of sailcloth, their hearts thumping. From their hiding place, Tom could see a wind-browned face, scored across with wrinkles and cracks like an old leather apron, its hair beneath the fur cap, grey and tattered. The man he guessed this must be the skipper. Then a second figure followed. This man was taller. His head was bare, the auburn hair crisply curling around a narrow foxy face. In his hand he held a dagger, a cool green stone in its hilt. His heavy woollen robe was topped by an embroidered surcoat with buttons of yellow bone and at his belt he wore a long slim blade in a jewelled scabbard.

Tom nudged Bessie in the darkness. 'He must be a knight,' whispered Tom. 'Ordinary people never wear swords.' There was no sign at all of the priests.

The wind-worn captain seemed strangely out of breath, his brow glistening with perspiration in spite of the wind and yet the sly-faced knight looked as cool as a crocodile. He threw back his head and laughed, his tongue glistening between pointed teeth.

'That was well done, Jonah! The poor fools have run straight into our trap. How were they to know the sailor who *just happened* to offer a passage to London worked for the man they'd followed all the way from Cairo?'

There was something distinctly evil in the knight's cold laugh. Tom shivered, pressing his face to a space between the rank-smelling sailcloth to get a better view. The captain dragged off his cap and used it to wipe his brow. 'If you'll beg pardon, Sir Jocelyn,' he said. 'It . . . it don't seem quite right to me . . . tying their hands like that, them being priests an' all . . .'

The wily knight's smile froze, his expression changing into a frown of astonishment. Jonah might be the best sea-captain this side of the channel but it was Sir Jocelyn who paid his wages. The captain would do well to know his place. 'Not quite right?' repeated Sir Jocelyn, his voice as chill as the blade of his dagger. 'Come now, Jonah. Since when have you had pangs of conscience? I don't pay you in gold for scruples!' He drew himself up to his full height and regarded the captain coldly, tapping his teeth slowly with the blade of his knife. As he did so, the lamplight gleamed on his silver finger. Bessie stifled a gasp.

Jonah puffed out his cheeks in a gesture of surrender. Sir Jocelyn did pay in gold – lots of it. He'd be a poorer man without the work the knight put his way. He shrugged his broad shoulders. 'What kind of priests are they anyway?' he said. 'I've never seen priests with brands on their for'eads before.'

'Never mind about the priests,' said the knight. 'I've got the casket back. That's what I came for.'

Tom dug Bessie hard in the ribs. *So he was right! The priests* had *stolen the golden casket!*

Sir Jocelyn frowned. 'This relic has proved more troublesome than any trade I've ever made,' he muttered to himself. 'But then this is no ordinary relic. Small wonder those priests followed me from Cairo to London to get their hands on it.'

'Whoever would have thought Caspar would betray the Three Wise Men?' said Jonah, interrupting the knight's reverie. 'After all you've been through together.'

Sir Jocelyn looked up sharply. 'To think that I evaded them all that way to England, only to be betrayed by that devil Caspar when I finally got it home!' he growled. 'I'd never have entrusted the relic to him for safekeeping if I thought he'd try to keep it for himself.'

Jonah pushed back his cap with a grunt of agreement. 'Well Caspar's certainly paid a heavy price.'

Sir Jocelyn gave a contemptuous laugh. 'Balthazar always did have the devil's own temper. Thank heavens I found out where Caspar had sent the casket before Balthazar dispatched him to the bottom of the Thames! A damned messy business though, and one that could still see us hang.' Sir Jocelyn's lip curled in distaste but nothing could spoil his good humour this evening. 'When I found out Caspar had sent the relic out of London, I'd a hunch I'd meet our dark-skinned friends in Saint Agnes Next-the-Sea. I didn't relish the prospect of breaking into Saint Wilfred's Abbey myself, I can tell you. But all I had to do was wait for them to do my dirty work for me. I always do have the luck of the devil when I sail on *Los Tres Magos*!'

Sir Jocelyn and the captain exchanged conspirators' smiles but the knight's eyes were anxious. He gazed out to sea across the choppy waves. 'Let's not count our rabbits before they're snared,' he said, a note of warning in his voice. 'This job's only half finished. Grab the tiller, Jonah. When you say the word, I'll loose the holding line.'

'The wind's getting up,' said Jonah. 'We'll hoist the sail when we've cleared the harbour wall.'

Bessie fought down a cry. 'They're casting off!' she breathed. Tom swallowed, pressing her cold fingers in the darkness.

'Hush!' he whispered. 'We can't show ourselves now. We've heard too much!'

There was a strong breeze and the black waves sparkled as the cog began to lurch through the sea, leaving the harbour wall far behind. The sea-captain raised his face to the scudding clouds. He licked his finger and held it up to the wind. 'There's a stiff north-easterly blowing now.'

'Set our course then, Jonah!' said Sir Jocelyn, bowing to the captain's greater knowledge of the ocean. 'Take us out to sea first and then we'll finish this business!'

He looked meaningfully at the captain. 'And no more scruples from you!'

The captain nodded. 'Whatever you say, Sir Jocelyn. After that we'll put in a tack and with the wind behind us we'll be sailing up the Thames estuary by sunrise.'

Tom gripped Bessie's hand. 'The Thames estuary!' he breathed, his fear tinged with excitement. 'We're going to London after all!'

Tom and Bessie heard the creak of the knight's retreating feet on the rungs of the ladder. He must be going down below. Through the chink in the sailcloth, they could still see the captain, astride at the helm, leaning his body into the tiller and staring up at the mast. For several minutes more they crouched in silence, listening to the crack of the sails and the whistle of the wind in the rigging and then all at once they heard a fearful sound that turned their blood to ice; the scrabble of feet on the ladder, the horrified jabbering of foreign tongues, then a spine-tingling scream as the priests were pushed onto the deck at knife-point, their hands bound fast behind their backs.

Bessie felt Tom shudder, and a ripple of raw fear passed from his body to hers and shivered down her spine. She clutched Tom's arm as Sir Jocelyn propelled the priests towards the side of the boat.

'What's happening, Tom?'

But before he had time to reply they heard a sickening sound, shrieks of inhuman terror, groans and grunts of an unequal struggle as Sir Jocelyn de Maltby tossed the bound priests, screaming for mercy, into the foaming sea.

Bessie couldn't stop herself. She let out a scream.

'What was that?' Sir Jocelyn's eyes flicked this way and that, raking the deck, his knuckles white on the dagger.

The captain's eyes darted at once towards the pile of sailcloth and Bessie's heart died within her. She could feel the rolling of the boat under her now as it rose and plunged to a wilder rhythm as the captain sprang from the helm and the tiller slammed hard to starboard. 'Over there!' cried Jonah. Bessie's stomach rose to her mouth. There was nowhere to run. They were trapped!

'Get a grip on the tiller, you fool!' roared the knight above the howl of the wind. 'You'll have us both overboard!' He was holding tight to the mast for support as the cog spun out of control. The captain hauled on the tiller and the ship lunged forwards again, lurching like a great animal through the dark.

Sir Jocelyn was breathing heavily. 'Probably just a rat,' he snarled, like a fox on the scent of baby rabbits. Following the captain's gaze, he crept towards the hiding place, 'But then again you . . . can . . . never . . . be . . . too *careful*!' And with a snarl he thrust his dagger into the pile of sailcloth, ripping the fabric aside with its cruel point. The smoky yellow light glinted on Sir Jocelyn's silver finger as he leaned over and grabbed Bessie Miller by the shoulder.

Bessie shrank back with a cry but there was nowhere to hide as the knight's face loomed over her, his lips drawn back in a snarl of astonishment. 'A rat it is!' he spat, hauling Bessie out by her arm. 'And I think it's a large one too!'

Bessie screamed, kicking and twisting in his iron grasp, thrashing like a landed fish and finally sinking her teeth into his hand. Sir Jocelyn roared in pain but still he held her fast. 'God's liver, it's a girl, Jonah! And a right little wild cat at that! Who the devil is she? What are you doing aboard *Los Tres Magos*?' he snarled in her face. 'What did you see?'

In an agony of indecision, Tom crouched in the shadows. As Sir Jocelyn had pulled back the sailcloth he'd rolled himself behind a barrel of salt-fish. He longed to spring to Bessie's aid. But then, what good could he be to her if he were captured as well? A knight armed with a dagger and sword would know how to use them. *Keep calm, Tom*, he told himself. *You can only help Bessie if they don't discover you're here.* She would think him a coward and yet he needed to keep his head and not succumb to his instinct to run blindly to help her. As long as they didn't hurt her, he had to stay hidden. Tom peered cautiously around the belly of the barrel, stretching his ears into the darkness.

Bessie felt sick with fear. *Where was Tom*?

The captain was looking troubled. 'What are we going to do with her?' asked Jonah. 'She's only a girl. Let's just tie her up, Sir Jocelyn, and take her down below.'

'Take her below?' scoffed Sir Jocelyn. 'I'm minded to throw her overboard with the priests and have done with the lot of them!' Bessie's knees were shaking uncontrollably. She squirmed and tried to wrench her arm away but Sir Jocelyn held her in a vice-like grip.

Jonah shook his head. 'You can't do that! I know a woman on board is bad luck but . . .'

'Exactly!' snarled Sir Jocelyn. 'A woman on board is a bad omen. And I've told you already. I have the devil's own luck when I sail on *Los Tres Magos*, and if you think

I'm risking that for this gypsy stowaway, I'm not the man with the silver finger!'

But the rough sea captain wouldn't budge. He'd seen enough violence for one night and though Sir Jocelyn paid his wages he knew he was the better sailor by a long way – and the knowledge gave him courage. Sir Jocelyn could never sail *Los Tres Magos* without him in such a wind.

'Them priests is one thing. This girl's another,' insisted Jonah with a thrust of his jaw. 'But I've a different idea.' He rubbed his thumb and forefinger together with a knowing smile. 'I think you'll be interested, Sir Jocelyn. I've got a friend what's leaving soon for North Africa. A girl like her would fetch a handsome price in the slave markets of Marrakech!'

Tom had to use all his self-control not to cry out. He could feel Bessie's fear, prickling under his skin.

Sir Jocelyn stroked his beard thoughtfully. 'Very well, Jonah,' he said at last. 'I dare say I could hide her at Balthazar's house whilst you arrange the details. But I can't keep her there for long. Now tell me,' he said with a twist of Bessie's arm. 'What sort of price could I expect for a white slave as pretty as the one I've got here?'

Tom had no idea how long he'd crouched after they had bound Bessie's hands and taken her down below. Numb with shock and the cold gnawing at his bones, he hardly dared breathe for fear he might give himself away. Bessie's screams from the hold wrenched at his heart. At last her cries grew weaker and then stopped altogether. Perhaps she'd exhausted herself. In some ways Tom was relieved.

He'd found the sound hard to bear and yet in another way he'd found it strangely comforting – a kind of connection with her.

And so they plunged on through the black ocean, the land like a dark mass on the starboard side, whilst cramped like a crab behind the barrel, Tom shook with rage. But his fury was mingled with relief. At least the captain's proposal had bought Bessie a little time. She was safe for a few more hours and now he had a clue about where they meant to take her when they finally reached London. *Balthazar's house.* Whatever he did, he mustn't forget that name!

Part Two

London

Chapter 10

The Bells of London

Los Tres Magos entered the Thames estuary as dawn turned the river to quicksilver. And with first light came the mournful cry of seabirds, following hungrily in their wake as the incoming tide carried them upstream towards the fabled city of London. It should have been a waking dream for Tom, who had never travelled farther than the horse fair in the next village. And yet his stomach churned with rising panic as the ancient Roman walls came into view and the bleak square silhouette of the Tower of London loomed grimly through the mist, guarding the eastern gate.

The skyline was thick with snow like a covering of almond paste on a yuletide pudding. So many steeples, so many spires – and a stone bridge across the river ahead of them, with houses along its broad span and a great stone chapel in the middle. *It must be a wicked city,* he thought, *to need so many churches.* Tom couldn't help gazing in wonder in spite of the danger he was in. He'd never seen so many ships. Sea-going cogs, flat-bottomed trading vessels, gilded barges . . .

The knight and the captain tied up at Fish Wharf, just downstream of London Bridge, to wait for the drawbridge to open. And it was then, as the silver sun rose weakly over the broad river that exhaustion caught up with Tom at last. Warmed a little by the sun and lulled by the rhythmic rocking of the boat on its mooring, Tom fell into a fitful sleep. Was he dreaming or did the great drawbridge open and the boat cast off again, sliding through the timber draw lock and into the upper reaches of the Thames? On he dozed, slipping in and out consciousness, as the captain moored *Los Tres Magos* at Queen's Hythe, that stinking wharf where all the fish in the city came ashore.

If it hadn't been for the point of a knife in her back, Bessie would have screamed for help as she was pushed up the narrow stairway and out into the watery sunlight of the deck, her hands bound tightly behind her, hidden beneath her cloak. Nor could she look around for any sign of Tom, since the knight had pulled her deep hood up over her head, so that she could only see straight in front of her, through a narrow chink in its thick folds. She could just see the captain, hurriedly checking the mooring lines, eager to be off. *Where in the world was Tom? Perhaps he was planning to follow when the coast was clear . . . that must be it!* He'd be sure to trail her, find out where this Balthazar lived and run and fetch help as soon as he could.

She shrank away in disgust at Sir Jocelyn's fierce breath

in her ear. 'Now you walk straight down that gangplank and keep your face covered, do you hear?' he snarled. 'One false move and you'll feel more than just the tip of my blade in your pretty neck!'

The ground still swayed, even as she stepped onto dry land, but the knight's fingers were steel on her arm. Bessie could feel the bruises spreading under her skin as he steered her roughly across the icy dockside away from the wharf. Her numb feet stumbled before her like puppet's feet, Sir Jocelyn pulling the strings. The Christmas bells began to peal and Bessie pressed her cold lips together, choking down a sob.

It was the sound of the bells that woke Tom, that and the warm sun on the back of his neck. He gave a violent start and scrambled to his knees. He peered over the side of the ship, blinking at the unfamiliar wharf with its wooden cranes like the necks of strange birds – and the river, so broad it made the River Twist seem only a trickling stream. *Where on earth was he?* And then with a sickening lurch of his stomach, he remembered Bessie.

Tom almost groaned aloud, cursing himself for falling asleep. He cringed back behind the salt-fish barrel, peering fearfully around its curving sides and out across the empty deck of *Los Tres Magos*. He held his breath and listened. They must all still be down below – probably asleep – resting after the night sail. But it was hard to hear anything above the noise. Every bell in the city must be ringing out for Christmas morning.

Way off downstream to the east, Tom could see the

massive bridge. The boat must have slipped through the drawbridge as he dozed. For the next few minutes Tom considered half a dozen ideas to help Bessie, dismissing them almost before they'd sprung into his head. Most of them involved creeping down into the hold and leaping on Sir Jocelyn from behind. But even in his desperation, he knew that would be futile. And anyway, there was the seaman to be reckoned with too. He'd probably get himself killed and Bessie into the bargain. No. However much he hated the idea, he had to stay hidden. What else could he do but watch and wait for them to come out?

On the harbour side, the river bank was a throng of merrymakers all wishing each other the blessings of the season. On the river side, a barge festooned with coloured ribbons floated past, a choir of boys from the great cathedral of Saint Paul, noses red and cheeks like apples, fluting a Christmas song. Tom knew the carol well. He had sung it with Brother Fergus in the choir at Saint Wilfred's. And with that memory, a lump rose in his throat. He had never felt more alone.

And then the realisation struck him like a bolt of lightning.

He *was* alone! Why hadn't he realised before? The deck of *Los Tres Magos* was bare, ropes neatly coiled in the stern and not a sound from below. Cautiously, Tom stole across the empty deck and peered down the ladder into the shadowy cabin. There was no candle light, no lantern . . . no sound of breathing. Holding his breath, he began to creep down the splintered rungs. He held his breath, scanning the empty room. Bessie and her captors had gone!

Tom fought down the panic that threatened to overwhelm him. He had kept a vigil for Bessie all night, only to doze off when she needed him most. What should he do? How long had she been gone? He had to think logically. Work out a plan. The sun was still low in the sky so surely it hadn't been long. He could try to find the sacrist of Westminster Abbey – the one who had given Abbot Fergus the casket for safekeeping. He'd be sure to help, once Tom told him where he'd come from and what had happened to the relic. And maybe the sacrist could tell him where to find the man they called Balthazar; it was hardly a common name. Of course he had no idea where the great Abbey of Westminster lay but he could always ask in the street. He gazed down at his clothes. All he had on was the hessian donkey costume, complete with tail! First things first. Before he could go any further, he needed some less ridiculous clothes.

Tom felt better now that he'd made a plan. His eyes scoured the gloomy space, his stomach clenched to a fist. He hoped he'd find something – perhaps some sailor's trousers and maybe even a cloak. He had to be quick. The captain and the knight could be back at any minute. There was an empty clay wine jar on a small rough table, and next to it, a calfskin telescope and a vellum map with a pair of dividers on top.

On the floor behind the table stood an iron-bound chest, a salt-rusted key in the lock. A strong musty smell of damp wool hit his nose as he lifted the lid. On the top, neatly folded, lay a sailcloth flag with the painted design of three golden crowns, a little cracked and weathered but clearly visible on the damp stiff fabric. As Tom hauled it out, his fingers stubbed against something hard that snagged as he pulled it, bringing with it a pair of woollen britches.

Tom didn't know whether to be more pleased with the britches or the small slim dagger, its bone handle engraved with the same golden crowns that he'd seen on the flag. In a flash, Tom was wriggling out of his hessian leggings and pulling on the baggy britches, completing his outfit with a moth-eaten jerkin of sheepskin that he'd dragged from the bottom of the trunk. The britches were several sizes too big but turned up at the bottom they would do very well. He pushed the dagger firmly into his waistband.

The noise of London was bad enough but nothing had prepared Tom for the smell as he stepped furtively from the stern of *Los Tres Magos* and onto the dock at Queen's Hythe. And the crowds! He had never seen so many people, even on market days in Saint Agnes, nor heard so many foreign tongues. The wharf was a stinking muddy place and as Tom stepped over a couple of wharfside cats fighting over a fish head, he realised it wasn't only the smell of fish that was making him feel queasy. For hanging above the tidal river were thirty separate seats in two straight rows, one row for men and one for women. His stomach heaved. The Thames was a common sewer!

Pinching his nose against the stink, Tom plunged quickly into the warren of crooked little streets that snaked back from the river. Cramped together trade by trade were the skinners, the saddlers, the embroiderers, the shoemakers, the goose-pluckers – all shut up for the holiday. However, the inns were full; more taverns than Tom had ever imagined could exist in one place together.

Tom hurried through the streets, turning this way and that, searching around for a friendly face to ask the way when he found he was back where he'd started. All the streets looked the same. With a fresh wave of panic he gazed anxiously around, hearing Abbot Fergus's voice in his head: *'London's a fearful place . . . full of thieves and beggars . . . all manner of evil lurking there . . .'* Well, at least he had nothing to fear from the pick-pockets, since he hadn't a penny to his name.

Passing by a cook shop, he gazed longingly at a string of roasting magpies twirling over a fire and his fingers began to twitch. His stomach ached with hunger. Would he dare? Shoot out a hand and snatch a sizzling magpie when the stall owner's back was turned?

Suddenly something hard stung Tom on the back of his neck, slithering wetly down his back. A perfect shot! He spun round with a startled cry to see where the slush-ball had come from. A small boy lounged grinning at him from the doorway of *The Dog's Head Tavern*, a filthy mongrel at his feet, a bright silk scarf tied round its neck.

'You look hungry,' said the boy, holding out a grubby hand. 'Bart's the name. And this 'ere dog's called Flea.'

Chapter 11

Bart and Flea

'Bartholomew Bucket's me full name but you can call me Bart,' smiled the boy, revealing a jumble of broken teeth. 'Bartholomew 'cos I was found on the steps of Saint Bartholomew the Great. That's a church, in case you don't know. And Bucket, 'cos that's what I was sleepin' in when I was took in.'

It was impossible to tell the boy's age. He was shorter than Tom, with a tangle of dirty black hair, skin as brown as a gypsy and an old-young face like a quizzical monkey with laughing eyes as black as ink and a cheeky cleft in his chin. Tom liked the look of him at once and when Flea leapt into Tom's arms and encircled his face three times with his large pink tongue, he knew he had met a friend.

The Dog's Head Tavern was lopsided and narrow and covered on the outside with carvings of dogs, and from a long splintered pole hung a badly painted sign of a snarling dog's head with two sharp rows of teeth. A dog, in fact, not in the least like Flea, who resembled nothing more than a dirty mop you might find abandoned on a midden heap; a vagabond sort of dog, at home in low taverns and dirty places but with a wide panting mouth that appeared to be smiling.

'Don't mind Flea,' said Bart over his shoulder, ducking under the densely carved lintel and beckoning Tom with a grimy finger. 'You oughta be flattered. He don't take to everyone like that. 'Specially not rats. It was a rat what tore 'is ear off see.' Bart clicked his fingers casually at the landlord who waved his hand and began to make his way across the filthy straw. 'Ale for two,' shouted Bart, 'and I'll 'ave me own tankard. The one with the silver rim!'

'A rat? Tore his ear off?' exclaimed Tom.

'Yeah! London rats is as big as cats, see.' Bart's eyes widened under his thick black brows that almost joined in the middle. 'It's all them dead bodies they gets to eat in the Thames. They grow huge and fat on the corpses they find floatin' there!'

Tom made a face. It was noisy in *The Dog's Head*, everyone sitting at low tables and shouting at one another whilst serving girls whirled past with platters of sizzling meats. He could almost taste the cheap tallow candles and he felt sure the rotting straw on the floor was alive with lice and fleas. Not a bit like *The Frisky Friar* with its fresh rushes scattered with sweet smelling herbs and where every face was known.

The Dog's Head was lit only by candles rammed into dusty old bottles that had grown over time into huge volcanoes of melted wax. The landlord slammed the tankards down in front of the boys, sloshing the ale on the sticky table. 'Keep the change,' swaggered Bart, flicking a short-cross penny in his direction. Tom's eyes widened in surprise. 'Me Pa's a knight, see,' said Bart, pouring some ale into his shoe for Flea to drink. Flea lapped it up quickly before it escaped through the holes. 'I jus' dress like this for fun. You get a bit sick of silks and satins after a bit. That's 'ow I got this tankard with a silver rim. I brought it back from the Holy Land. I went with me father on Crusade. He's a knight an' all!'

'You've been to Palestine?' asked Tom incredulously. It was a far cry from being found in a bucket! 'I've always wanted to go there. Our old abbot went on Crusade. What's it like?'

'S'all right,' shrugged Bart. 'Not as good as Constanti-what-not, is it Flea?'

'You've been to Constantinople as well?' gasped Tom.

'Course I 'ave! Everyone there wears cloth made of gold. Even the fishermen!' He slurped his beer and wiped his mouth on his sleeve. 'That's better,' he said with a smack of his lips. 'Thames ale made from Thames water.'

'Thames water! But it's filthy. And what about the corpses?'

'We gets us water when the tide's out and the fresh water's flowing downstream,' grinned Bart. 'You need to remember that if you're gonna survive in London. Only drink the water when the tide's out!' Tom took a cautious swig of ale. It tasted thin and sour, as if every washerwoman in London had used it first. Bart shot him a crooked smile. 'Not from these parts, then?' he said.

'Er . . . no . . . not at all,' stammered Tom, thinking fast. He didn't know Bart from Adam himself but then again, he didn't know anyone else either and the boy seemed friendly enough. 'Look. You might be able to help me. I'm looking for somebody. She's in terrible trouble. I don't know London and I need to find Westminster Abbey quickly. There's somebody there I need to speak to . . .'

Bart's shoulders broadened. 'Well, you've come to the right person then, hasn't he Flea? Me dad's the Abbot of Westminster Abbey! I can take you there with me eyes shut.'

'But . . . but he can't be your father,' protested Tom. 'Abbots don't have children. They're supposed to be celibate. And anyway, I thought your father was a knight.'

Bart looked Tom straight in the eye. 'Yeah well, it's a bit complicated, see. The *knight* now, he's me step-father. Me *real* father's the abbot but he couldn't own up to it. So he give me to the knight to avoid a scandal!'

Tom scratched his head. Now he was *really* confused. 'But I thought you were found in a bucket . . . on the steps of Saint Bartholomew's church . . .'

'That's right,' said Bart without a moment's hesitation. 'It was the *abbot* what left me in the bucket – and the priest at Saint Bart's give me a name and then handed me over to the knight what took me to Palestine. So now you know all about me. But I don't know nuffink about you.'

The icy snow crunched under Bessie's feet as the knight steered her up one crooked alley and down another between lopsided houses that almost met overhead. Beggars rubbed their eyes in doorways and chestnut sellers began to coax their braziers into life as small points of candlelight bobbed behind wattle shutters in the dingy streets. Before long they passed under the shadow of a monstrous double-towered prison in the city wall and were soon on a wider road leading west out of London. Shaking back her hood as much as she dared, Bessie saw stone halls, not unlike the merchants' houses of Saint Agnes, but very much grander. The beggars and chestnut sellers had been replaced by fashionably dressed people scurrying by, muffled against the cold. No one would ever have guessed that the girl with the elegant knight by her side walked with a knife in her back.

Bessie was so tired she felt she might faint, and as fear gave way to exhaustion, she began to give up hope. How would Tom ever find her now, even if he had managed to give the captain the slip? They had walked so far and through such winding streets that she'd long ago lost track of the route. Suddenly, the knight came to an abrupt halt before a pair of iron gates adorned with a coat of arms with three distinctive golden crowns and topped with a row of wicked-looking spikes that opened into a cobbled courtyard. Even with her limited vision, Bessie could tell that this was a large mansion. It must belong to someone important if the coat of arms was anything to go by. A distant bell rang somewhere deep within and then she was stumbling on again, skirting the heavy stone balustrades and around to the rear of the house. Bessie had little time to take in her surroundings before she was pushed through a back door and into a low roofed passage and down a small flight of shallow stairs.

'Move, damn you!' hissed Sir Jocelyn in her ear.

'W . . . where am I? Where are you taking me?' Bessie's voice trembled but there was fury deep in her heart. *How dare the knight treat her this way?* The passage reeked of damp like an underground cave and there was a strong odour of tallow from rush flares on the walls. She felt sick and dizzy. And then the bonds that bound her wrists were roughly removed and with a final shove she pitched forward onto the damp floor of a low-beamed room. There was just time to take in a pyramid of barrels at one end before the door slammed shut behind her and in a clatter of bolts she became a prisoner once more.

Bessie knew it was hopeless, yet still she flung herself again and again against the iron-studded door. Shaking with rage, she groped in vain for a handle, raking with her nails across the splintery surface. But there was no latch, not even a keyhole. With trembling fingers, she groped at her neck for the charm ribbon – holly berries, juniper and mistletoe – and with a howl of fury, she wrenched it from her neck and flung it at the door. Her mother had been right. What use were her spells? What use had they ever been? Tears of rage and misery flowed unchecked down Bessie's cheeks. Tom would never find her here!

Chapter 12

The Soporific Sponge

Christmas morning and the abbey was a hive of speculation as rumours buzzed from dormitory to cloister and back again. *Abbot Fergus had been stabbed. He'd been hit from behind with a golden chalice. He was dead. He was alive. He lay unconscious with a wound in his head.* The monks were worse than the novices, a-twitter with half-truths and far-fetched tales. The only certainty was that Tom Fletcher had disappeared like a puff of incense – and the miller's girl with him. And in a dimly lit room in Saint Wilfred's infirmary, Brother Silas, the physician, was explaining about the soporific sponge.

'You had a lucky escape,' he told Abbot Fergus, who lay propped up in bed in the infirmary, his face as white as the linen sheet, his dog by his side. 'You were drugged. The sponge your attacker used was infused with a heady mixture: hemlock, henbane, mandragora and the poppy of sleep.'

'Poppy of sleep!' croaked the physician's Caladrius, fluttering its white wings from its perch on his shoulder. Abbot Fergus eyed the bird suspiciously. Brother Silas had taught the hideous creature to talk since the summer. The physician had better not try the bird's talents out on him. The last time Silas had used the Caladrius to predict life and death, old Abbot Theodore had died!

Brother Silas lifted the offending wad of cloth from the table and sniffed delicately, his nostrils a-quiver. 'Yes. This is definitely mandragora – and the gall of a castrated boar, if my nose does not deceive me. I know the recipe well. We used it in Salerno for amputations when I was a medical student nearly forty years ago. Arabic in origin of course – like all the best medicine.

'Now, hold still whilst I apply this poultice to your head. Wood Betony mixed with hog's lard to help the wound knit clean. You gave yourself quite a knock when you fell. If Mungo hadn't found you and barked the alarm, you might well have bled to death!'

Abbot Fergus winced as the poultice made contact with the open wound. Mungo whined in sympathy. 'Any news of Brother Thomas?' asked the abbot faintly, as if inquiring for the first time. In fact he had asked about nothing else all morning, his eyes darting hopefully to the door at the slightest sound in the corridor. 'I'm quite sure he'll turn up soon,' he added. 'It's not the first time he's gone missing and he always comes back in the end.' He frowned heavily and passed an anxious hand through his stormy red hair.

'I have told you already, Abbot,' replied Brother Silas. 'I'll let you know just as soon as there's anything to report.

Now try and get some sleep. If I am correct about the soporific sponge, you'll need the best part of Christmas Day to sleep it off.'

Abbot Fergus nodded weakly and closed his eyes, his brow creased in pain, though not of a kind to be soothed away by hogs' grease. He could remember nothing of the night before, except a mahogany brown arm snaking around his neck before he fell. And now he knew that the mysterious casket was gone; the one he had been entrusted to keep safe by Brother Gideon of the great Abbey of Westminster. He'd asked Brother Silas to check the sacristy the moment he'd woken up. And even worse than that, Brother Thomas had disappeared too – or so he'd been told.

The abbot was strangely confused about the casket. On the one hand, he felt an overwhelming sense of loss as if some precious part of him had been torn away leaving the wound still raw. And yet at the same time, he felt oddly relieved in spite of everything. He'd known no peace since he had set eyes on the relic – and now it was gone he felt as if a burden had been lifted away. So it was not for loss of the casket that his hollow eyes were even now filling with tears. *Could what Brother Dunstan was saying be true*? *Tom Fletcher guilty of the crime!* They had found his donkey's head covered in a thick layer of snow under the broken sacristy window. Had it really been Tom's arm that had snaked around his neck, stained with walnut juice from the play? Brother Thomas, his favourite novice? And after all they had been through!

Abbot Fergus's eyes shot open again at a sharp knock on the door. And as if conjured up by the abbot's thoughts, the novice master scurried in, his obsequious face a study of barely suppressed delight. Brother Thomas had thumbed his nose at the rules of the abbey once too often. Well, now he was exposed for the villain that he was.

'I told you he was the rotten herring in the barrel!' cried Brother Dunstan triumphantly, backing away from Mungo who had risen to his feet, hackles raised. The Caladrius made a lunge for the novice master with its hooked beak, as if to show solidarity with the dog. 'As leader of the novices, I should know,' continued Brother Dunstan, batting the bird away with his hand. 'But no one would pay me any heed.' He glanced over his shoulder and beckoned to Odo and Felix who were hovering eagerly in the corridor outside. 'Now come along in boys and show Abbot Fergus what you have just shown me.'

The boys shuffled in exchanging sneaky glances, Odo holding a piece of parchment by the corner as if it might bite and Felix, twitching with excitement like a dog with the fleas. But no sooner had the two novices crossed the threshold than another rumpus sounded in the corridor and the quill master hurtled in, his round pink face awash with anxious perspiration. He tried to push in front of the novice master, pulling a tearful Edmund behind him by the hand. Then everybody spoke at once:

'We found a note under Tom's bolster . . .'

'He's run away to London . . .'

'He never meant to take his vows . . .'

'Yes, he did!'

'No he didn't!'

Abbot Fergus clapped his hand to his already pounding

head. 'Silence all of you! I'd get more sense out of a gaggle of geese! Now, Brother Dunstan. Since you were here first . . .'

Brother Ambrose glared furiously at the novice master. Brother Dunstan gave a self-important cough. 'As we all know,' he began, 'a donkey's head belonging to Brother Thomas was found by the broken sacristy window . . .'

'And now we've found a note . . .' interrupted Felix, unable to contain himself any longer.

'Under his bolster in the dormitory,' crowed Odo, waving the parchment in the air. 'It's from the miller's daughter. They were planning to run away to London!'

Abbot Fergus collapsed inside like a punctured wineskin. So it *was* true! He had heard the miller's girl was missing. Sir Ranulf de Lacy and the miller had been up at the abbey early this morning asking questions and with the news that a quantity of money had disappeared from the miller's home at Tirley Grange. Now here, it seemed, was the proof. He shook his head sadly as he read the letter, his lips mouthing the scribbled words ' . . . *after the novices' play . . . under the rose window . . . bring whatever you can lay hands on . . . might be our only chance to get away! Bessie.*' Abbot Fergus sank back on his bolster with a moan, the letter fluttering from his hand and landing on the floor by his bed.

Brother Ambrose sprang to his side, scooping it up. 'We are surely jumping to conclusions,' he pronounced, crumpling the parchment in his hand. 'Maybe Brother Thomas has fled to London to avoid taking his vows but that alone does not make him guilty of assault and theft. But listen! You are not the only ones with news. Brother Edmund has something to tell which might shed some light on the matter. Come, Edmund,' he said with a nod of encouragement, pushing the small boy forward. 'Speak up.'

All eyes now turned on Ed, who was blushing to the roots of his hair. He licked the stubs of his two front teeth. 'I . . . I saw two brown-skinned monks with eyes as black as . . . as damsons,' he lisped. 'They were hiding in the hay loft when I went to fetch the manger for the play. I told everyone about it in the barn but not even Tom believed me. He said I must have seen the Brown Boggart! *You* remember, Odo,' he cried, his eyes wide with conviction. '*You* were there . . . and Felix too! Herbert even came with me to look in the hay loft!'

Abbot Fergus glanced sharply at Odo and Felix. 'Is this true, boys? I confess I have been troubled by a strange sensation of being watched ever since I arrived from London. For the love of God, speak up if this is true!'

But Odo's prim little mouth was tight as a wrinkle. He glanced slyly at Felix. 'It's a lie!' burst out Felix. 'He never said a word about any brown monks, did he Odo?'

Ed let out a strangled cry but Brother Dunstan silenced him with a glare as Odo leant towards Abbot Fergus with a simper. 'Not a word, I'm afraid, Abbot.'

Abbot Fergus glared at Odo. 'And what about Herbert?' he asked coldly. 'Did *he* see these monks?' but when he turned his head to look at Ed, the abbot's tone was gentle. 'Why is Herbert not here?'

Ed's face, already pink, flushed scarlet. He opened his mouth and then closed it again. 'They . . . there was nobody there when we went back to look,' he admitted, staring dismally down at his boots. 'So Herbert didn't see anything, I'm afraid.'

Brother Dunstan turned from Ed with a snort of disdain. 'So everything slots into place!' he crowed. 'A missing novice who doesn't want to take his vows. A note that tells of his plans to escape taking "anything he can lay his hands on". I only repeat the words of the note, you understand. A broken sacristy window. A precious casket is missing. It points in only one direction!'

'But surely you are forgetting the soporific sponge,' protested Abbot Fergus, his faith in Tom still hanging by a thread. 'Brother Silas has explained that I was overcome by the "poppy of sleep". How would young Thomas know how to create something like that? Perhaps our physician could tell us?' he said looking at Brother Silas, a note of appeal in his voice.

Brother Silas cleared his throat awkwardly. He had never had much time for Tom Fletcher, although since the events of the summer he had allowed him a grudging respect. On the other hand, he loathed Brother Dunstan. He sighed regretfully. There was nothing else to be done. 'I am sorry to say that he knew the ingredients all too well,' confessed Silas with a rueful twist of his mouth. 'He watched me make a draught of it before the bonesetter set the arm that he broke last summer.'

'What more proof do we need?' cried the novice master in triumph.

But the quill master had one more question. 'Abbot Fergus. This precious casket that you say has been stolen,' he ventured, ignoring Brother Dunstan's poisonous glance. 'Did anyone else know it was in the abbey before it was stolen last night? Had you shown it to anyone?'

They could have heard a feather fall. Abbot Fergus stared hard at the kindly quill master, tears of hurt in his eyes. Tom had been his soul mate, his chief chorister, his loyal friend and yet Fergus was abbot now, and he could not tell a lie. He raked a weary hand through his hair with a heavy heart. 'There *was* someone else who knew of the casket,' he said at length. 'Tom Fletcher.'

Brother Dunstan's whoop was jubilant. 'He will hang for this!' he cried. 'Theft and attempted murder!'

'No!' screamed Ed. Brother Ambrose sprang towards the novice master, his face contorted with rage.

'No wait!' he cried, surprising even himself at his ferocity. 'Our novice master is surely forgetting that priests are never executed for their crimes. Brother Thomas will be tried in the Church Court, not by the common law.' He took a step towards Edmund who was now weeping silently and placed a comforting hand on his arm. 'Brother Dunstan has never liked Tom Fletcher,' said the quill master in icy tones, 'but he is mistaken this time. Even if the boy is guilty of these crimes – and nothing is yet proven – we will still not see him hanged!'

But victory was Brother Dunstan's. 'No, Ambrose,' he said softly, his smile like the blade of a knife. 'It is *you* who are mistaken. The benefit of the Church Courts is for those of us who are ordained priests. Tom Fletcher did not take his vows, as all of us know. *Novice* he may be but *monk* he most certainly is not. Well, now he will pay the price!'

* * *

Up in the novices' dormitory, Herbert sat dejectedly on his straw pallet, his head in his hands. He had searched in vain for Tom last night after Ethelwig's star had exploded during the play, fearful that Tom had been hurt in the fire and was lying injured somewhere and needing his help. All night as rumours about Tom flew back and forth around the cloisters, he had furiously defended his best friend's honour, indignantly refusing to believe that Tom had anything to do with the attack on Abbot Fergus. Even when the donkey's head had been found earlier this morning in a snow drift under the sacristy window, Herbert had tried to explain it away.

But this letter was the final straw! What was he to think now; now that they'd found the note from Bessie under Tom's bolster? For the first time since Tom had disappeared, Herbert's loyalty had begun to falter. He frowned. Perhaps he didn't really know Tom at all. He'd been acting very strangely of late and there'd been a cooling in their friendship.

Herbert sniffed and pressed his fingers into his eyes. It wouldn't do for the other novices to come back and find him crying. He'd never live that one down with Odo and Felix. He shook his head despondently, wishing with all his heart that he could have gone along with Ed to see Abbot Fergus and backed up his story about the black-eyed priests. But how could he, when he knew the hay loft had been empty? And so he'd stayed away from the infirmary and Odo and Felix's spiteful tongues.

Herbert groaned and got up from his pallet, pulling

his robe down over his plump stomach. *Had Tom really stolen from the sacristy leaving Abbot Fergus for dead? Abbot Fergus whom Tom adored?* Herbert shook his head angrily, wiping his eyes on the sleeve of his robe. He couldn't . . . he *wouldn't* believe what they were saying! He gazed defiantly at Tom's empty pallet, its bolster askew to the floor where Odo had flung it in his delight at finding the note. Herbert could see very well that the evidence pointed at Tom. But he knew in his heart they were wrong! There *had* to be another explanation. Tom was innocent! He was certain of it!

Over at Tirley Grange, Alice Miller gingerly pushed open the door of Bessie's room. It was foolish, she knew, after a fruitless night spent searching for her, and yet a ghost of a hope was still there. She could smell a faint aroma of her daughter, the musky smell of damask roses that Bessie soaked patiently in oil to extract the exotic perfume. With a trembling step, Alice crossed into the room, blinking at the brightness of the early morning light. The shutters had not been closed on Christmas Eve and now the dazzling snow outside reflected back from the white ceiling. The woollen curtains were drawn around the new timber-framed bed with its feather-filled mattress.

A tear trembled on the edge of her eyelid then fell with a splash onto her hand. Feathers, not straw for Bessie! She knew she had spoiled her daughter, loving her too fiercely, like many a mother of an only child. She placed a trembling hand on the woollen fabric of the bed curtain. For the hundredth time in her mind she wrenched back the drapes to find that Bessie was there after all, a sleepy mound of tangled black hair. And Alice imagined herself kneeling by the bed, gathering Bessie to her breast, telling her that everything would be all right. She would explain to Sir Ranulf . . . and Baron Godric would be gone . . .

Gently, she pulled back the curtain. Alice had seen it before but still the tears sprang to her eyes at the sight of the empty mattress with Bessie's straw doll on the pillow, the one with the woollen hair that Alice had sewn in herself. Alice's tears began to flow anew from under her swollen eyelids as she dropped to her knees by the bed, her hands pressed to her face. Clutching the doll to her chest, she rocked backwards and forwards and then with a sudden groan of despair she flung it violently away from her. It whirled in the air, turned a pretty somersault, its skirt billowing, and landed neatly on the wide stone sill just as the muffled sound of a horse's hooves clopped over the frost-hardened snow.

Alice flew to the window, her heart full of hope and stared down into the yard. *Bessie would be with her father, up on the horse, her sleepy arms around Gabriel's waist!* But Gabriel's broad shoulders were hunched, head sunk down on his chest in despair. As he approached the house, he raised his weary eyes towards Bessie's casement. Was he praying to see his daughter hanging out, waving the news that all was well or did he know deep inside that only Alice would be there? Meeting his wife's expectant gaze, he briefly shook his head and Alice could see that the rough old miller was crying too.

Chapter 13

The Cockertrice

' 'ere,' said Bart, tearing a leg off the chicken that was steaming on the table between them and offering it to Tom. ' 'ave a chew on that. Can't think straight when your stomach's best friends wiv yer backbone!'

Tom accepted the chicken leg gratefully. After all, he told himself with a stab of guilt, what good would it do Bessie if he went hungry? Bart tore off the other leg for himself and ate greedily.

'Now let's get this clear in me 'ead,' he said when he'd finished, tossing the bone to Flea who caught it with an expert leap. 'You're a runaway novice what's lookin' for yer friend what's been took by a man wiv a silver finger . . . the one what threw the priests over the side of the boat . . .'

The ale had loosened Tom's tongue, and once he'd started his tale, he felt almost dizzy with the relief of finding a friend to share his trouble. 'So that's why I need to see the sacrist of Westminster Abbey,' finished Tom hurriedly.

'He gave the casket I told you about to the abbot of *my* abbey to keep safe. Maybe he'll know the knight with the silver finger and even who Balthazar is. Can you take me there now?'

Bart took a slug of ale and wiped his mouth on his sleeve before shaking his head.

'Why not?' said Tom hotly. 'If you know the way to the abbey with your eyes shut . . .'

'Oh I know the way all right,' shrugged Bart. 'But it wouldn't do you no good to see 'im now. He's dead see. He was found at the bottom of Dead Man's Stairs the other day. Some say he did 'imself in. But that's not what most people think. People are sayin' he was murdered!'

'Murdered?' gasped Tom, jumping up and knocking over his stool. Flea skittered across the rushes with an indignant yelp. Tom picked up his stool and sat back down with a frown. After all, this was probably just another of Bart's tall tales. 'How was he murdered?' asked Tom suspiciously. 'Why didn't you say so before?'

'Strangled!' said Bart. 'Or drowned! When they pulled 'im out of the river, all stinkin' and bloated, they found a cord wound right round 'is neck!' Bart nodded vigorously at Tom. 'Honest! It's true. Ask anyone here.'

Tom felt the ground shift, and this time it wasn't because of the ale. *What was the secret of this casket? Abbot Fergus had been so peculiar about it. The dark-skinned priests had stolen it. The knight had killed the priests for it. And now the sacrist of Westminster Abbey, who gave it to Fergus in the first place, seemed to have died a horrible death.* Tom was feeling slightly sick already with the ale and the stink of cheap tallow candles. And now the image of the bloated corpse of the sacrist was causing his stomach to heave.

'Listen, Bart!' said Tom urgently. The mention of the drowning had suddenly reminded him. 'Where is this Dean Man's Stairs? Is it on the River Thames?'

Bart snorted rudely. 'Course it is, you noodle! Everyone's heard of Dead Man's Stairs! It's where all the corpses come to rest.'

Tom caught his breath. *There had to be a connection! Hadn't the knight, Sir Jocelyn, said something about somebody drowning in the Thames?* Tom bit his lip trying to remember. *The knight was talking about the casket. Then the ship's captain said something like:* 'Whoever would have thought Caspar would betray the three wise men?' *And then something about how they'd discovered where Caspar had sent the casket before he'd ended up at the bottom of the Thames!*

Tom pushed back his stool in alarm. 'What's the sacrist of Westminster Abbey called?' he asked suddenly. 'I bet his name's Caspar!'

But Bart seemed to have lost interest in Tom and his problems and was busy adjusting the scarf around Flea's grubby neck. He gave a huge yawn. 'He weren't called Caspar or anyfink fancy like that,' he said finally. 'His name was Brother Gideon.'

Oh. Tom put his face in his hands, despair washing over him like the incoming tide. The sacrist of Westminster had been his only hope. He'd failed Bessie completely. He had to find her soon – before they shipped her off to Marrakech. But looking for Bessie in this vast city would be like trying to strike gold in a tin mine. Where should he begin? Who else did he know?

'So who else do you know what could 'elp you find yer friend?' said Bart as if reading Tom's thoughts. 'You could go the coroner, I suppose, or the sheriff and tell 'em what you seen . . .'

Tom looked up sharply. It must have been the mention of authority that jogged Tom's memory, for he suddenly heard a high pitched bray in his head and the vision of a horse-faced Justice floated into his mind, a strutting peacock of a lawyer with cruel green eyes. 'Well, now you mention it,' he said slowly. 'There is someone I *sort of* know.'

Sir Percy FitzNigel, Justice to the King, was expecting company in his intimate dining room, up a short flight of stairs from the grand solar. A blazing fire roared in the hearth where Humphrey Pickerel, his pinch-faced servant, was roasting a crane on a skewer. Its serpentine neck, even longer than Sir Percy's own, was wound three times around a spit and curved backwards in a graceful arch until its beak came to rest on its sizzling breast. Golden light from rush torches gleamed on the buckles of the Justice's soft leather boots and sparkled on the jewelled collar of his silver-grey hound as Sir Percy flicked a speck of dust from his linen tunic, embroidered with silver stars.

He surveyed the Christmas table, licking his fleshy lips in satisfaction. All was prepared: the trenchers of beaten silver, the beeswax candles, the golden bowl of exotic fruits that tumbled in profusion, spilling onto the crisp damask cloth. And the centrepiece – a Cockertrice; a curious beast, half-flesh, half-fowl, with the foreparts of a capon and the hind parts of a piglet, stuffed with goose livers and cumin seeds and stitched back together with a silver thread. Too much food, some might have said, for a dinner for two.

'A great pity about Sir Henry de Mandeville, don't you agree, Porpoise?' brayed Sir Percy, raising his goblet to the pallid servant who was forlornly scratching his chilblains between cranks of the spit handle. They had just received news that the Chief Justice was, once more, indisposed.

'The name is Pickerel,' corrected the servant, giving the roasted crane an extra hard crank, imagining its neck was Sir Percy's.

'It's his old stomach trouble again, Pilchard!' said Percy, with an artificial smile. 'It's too bad that sweet Mabel and I will have to dine alone. I have sent him a jar of my autumn honey from the new hives. Poor fellow. He cannot cling onto the post of Chief Justice for many months longer. It's time for him to stand down and make room for a younger man!'

He smiled to himself. A word in the Chief Justice's ear from his daughter might make all the difference. Mabel de Mandeville was a silly wench but plump as a partridge and with eyes as blue as speedwells. She would suit him very well. He flung himself down in a high backed chair and caught up his lute. Perhaps a tender ballad would complete the romantic effect of the meal. Mabel might hear it as she crossed the courtyard, although the air was too chill to open up the casement. He would have to sing loudly to be heard through the glass.

'Listen to this one, Porpoise!' he cried. 'I composed it

myself.' He twanged his ill-tuned lute and began to warble in a thin jarring voice, his green eyes closed in rapture.

'Take thou this rose, O rose,
Since love's own flower it is,
And by that rose, O rose,
Thy lover captive is.

'I think she'll like it, don't you, Porpoise? How do I look by the way? Clean shaven in the European manner with just a touch of cochineal paste to my cheeks. You could use some yourself, come to think of it!'

'A little expensive, Sir Percy,' he replied tartly, 'on a salary of tuppence a day.'

A high-pitched scream rent the frosty air in the courtyard outside. Sir Percy sprang to the window almost dropping his lute, but by the time he reached it the commotion had transferred itself to the short flight of stairs to the dining room, and was proceeding upwards in a tirade of abuse.

'Take your foot off my gown, Sparrow, or I will box your ears!' cried Mabel de Mandeville, tossing her flaxen braids in ill-temper and rearranging the circlet of winter roses on her head. She made a rush at her maidservant, her sharp fists clenched, as the elderly creature, grey jowls a-wobble, shuffled up the stairs gathering the hem of her mistress's robe.

'P . . . pardon me for saying so, Mabel, but 'tis your own foot on the gown,' stammered the old chaperone, barely raising her head from the step. 'If you would simply raise your heel . . .'

'Hold your tongue, Sparrow!' Mabel retorted, aiming a kick at the maid's head. 'If I say you're treading on my gown . . . *then you're treading on my gown*! Oh, Sir Percy! There you are,' she squealed, showing her neat white teeth in a good-humoured smile.

Sir Percy waggled his fingers in greeting.

'Father thanks you for the honey,' simpered Mabel from under her eyelashes as Sir Percy ushered her into the dining room. She gazed about her. 'This is very intimate, Percy,' she giggled. Then arranging her features into an expression of regret, she added, 'Poor Father. He doesn't seem any better at all.' Then catching sight of the Cockertrice on the silver platter, she screeched like a parrot, seizing Sir Percy's arm with a shiver of horror. 'What in the world is that, Percy dear? It looks like something from the King's Beast House in The Tower!'

Sir Percy laughed a huge braying laugh. 'Just a savoury innovation from my new Venetian cook, my dear. Only the best for the Chief Justice's pretty daughter! Such a pity your father is unwell yet again and on Christmas Day too.' He hesitated, his eyes glittering a venomous green. 'I wonder . . . has he ever mentioned retiring to you?'

Chapter 14

Mulberry Pudding

Bart seemed to know where they might find FitzNigel Hall. 'Close by Westminster Abbey, I 'fink it should be,' said Bart confidently. 'That's where all them lawyers are movin' to now – to be near the law courts in Westminster Hall. I'll show you the abbey and then we can ask anybody you like the way from there.'

So Tom had followed Bart and Flea from *The Dog's Head Tavern*, down the slippery hill from Saint Paul's, its spire pointing skywards like a giant icicle and out through the city wall at Ludgate. Bart walked on ahead, so quickly Tom had to jog to catch up. It had begun to snow again, great grubby flakes like feathers from an old split mattress. *Even the snow is dirty in London*, thought Tom gloomily. The streets were lit by torches, although it was still daytime, their rosy flames lighting up the shop signs. Every so often Tom's stomach would flip at a glimpse of black curls at a turn in an alley and he'd break into a run, shrinking back as an unknown face turned indignantly at his tap on the shoulder.

Before long they were crossing the wooden bridge that spanned the icy River Fleet, Bart pointing out churches left and right, the doors festooned with garlands for Christmas Day. Tom was overwhelmed. 'One hundred and twenty-six churches within the city wall,' Bart had boasted proudly, exclaiming in disbelief when Tom told him Saint Agnes had only one.

They had been squelching through the slush for almost an hour when the grey bulk of Westminster Abbey loomed into view, with the little church of Saint Margaret, nestling like a newly hatched chick, next to its larger parent. And from there a red-nosed ferryman pointed the way.

This is a fool's errand, thought Tom as he followed Bart. *What if Sir Percy won't see me . . . ? What if he does see me . . . ? What will I say to him?* The truth was he didn't exactly *know* the Justice and the Justice certainly didn't know him. Tom had seen him at Saint Agnes; it was nothing more than that.

'We'd best go round the back,' said Bart under his breath as the house loomed into view. 'Gentlefolks don't take too kindly when the likes of me come knockin' at the front. They think I must be beggin'.'

FitzNigel Hall had sumptuous rooms with windows of costly glass, and it was from one of these casements that a great bray of laughter reached their ears along with the distinctive smell of roasting fowl. Tom gazed up at the lighted window, a sinking feeling in his stomach, wishing with all his heart that he'd never come.

* * *

Under the kissing bough of holly and bay that hung from a beam above the table, Sir Percy FitzNigel offered his wine-stained lips to Mabel de Mandeville's rosebud mouth. 'Romance is in my nature,' he declared flirtatiously. 'I was born under the sign of Venus, not Virgo you understand. I was born for love, not the cloister!'

The Chief Justice's daughter giggled, her mouth too full of mulberry pudding to reply. She swallowed noisily, emitting small grunts of pleasure as she chewed. Sir Percy reached for her hand and before she could withdraw it, he raised it to his lips, tasting the sticky fingers, one by one. It was a bold move, even for Sir Percy, but the strong French wine was throbbing in his veins. So it was no surprise that he didn't hear the knocking on the door.

'Begging your pardon, Sir Percy,' said Humphrey Pickerel. 'There's someone to see you in the back yard.'

Sir Percy reluctantly uncoiled his arm from around the thick waist of the Chief Justice's daughter. 'But it is Christmas Day!' he exclaimed. 'Tell whoever it is to be off. Tell them the Chief Justice is busy! I . . . I mean . . . forgive me, Mabel,' stammered Sir Percy, caught for a moment off guard, 'just a slip of the tongue. I meant . . . inform whoever is pestering me that the *King's* Justice is otherwise engaged.'

Humphrey Pickerel bent towards the Justice's ear and whispered. Sir Percy tossed his head like an impatient horse. 'All right! All right! I'll come in a moment. You must excuse me, Mabel,' he said with a swagger. 'You cannot rise to my position without being plagued by public business whatever the day might be. Tell the wretches I'm coming – just as soon as I've finished my meal.'

So whilst Sir Percy finished his mulberry pie, Tom waited anxiously with Bart in the icy back yard, blowing on his blue fingers and watching some servants playing Snap Dragon. But Tom had no stomach for games today, so he motioned to Bart to move off and they sat on the rim of a newly constructed well, scooping up snow and sending ice balls tumbling down onto the frozen surface while they waited.

It was Flea who announced the arrival of Sir Percy, flying joyfully to greet the elegant hound at his heels as if they were old friends. 'Call that filthy vermin off my dog!' cried the King's Justice, reeling back and seizing his own hound's jewelled collar to restrain it from joining the fun. He kicked out at Flea with his leather boots but the vagabond dog was too quick. And as Flea ducked and dodged between the Justice's legs, he exchanged good natured nips with Sir Percy's greyhound. All of which did not put Sir Percy in the best temper for listening to two scruffy urchins, one of whom claimed to be a runaway novice from a coastal abbey he'd visited for the autumn assizes.

In fact the interview could not have gone worse for Tom. Sir Percy, puffed up like an indignant cockerel, was not to be disturbed from his wooing. Didn't they know it was Christmas Day? The courts were not sitting and everyone was making merry. And anyway, he had not the least interest in some tawdry relic from a coastal abbey. Surely there were enough fragments of the true cross in the city's churches to build another bridge over the River

Thames! And what were two foreign priests and a chit of a miller's daughter to him? Lord, who did they think he was? A village constable in charge of the hue and cry? There were two sheriffs and a coroner in the city – so why come bothering him? And as for a murderous knight with a silver finger. Well, Sir Percy had never heard of such a fellow. They'd been listening to too many folk tales, in his view, or drunk too many tankards of festive ale.

Tom turned sadly away, feeling utterly dejected. What a naïve fool he was to have thought the cruel-eyed Justice would help him. He'd not even had chance to mention Balthazar. But as he and Bart made their way back across the icy yard they heard a high pitched cry from a lighted casement. 'You there!' shouted Sir Percy from the window. 'The one with the mangy dog!'

Bart turned sharply and scurried back, Flea at his heels. To Tom's surprise he saw Sir Percy toss a small object down to Bart from the window. A brief exchange of words and Bart came hurrying back clutching a cloth pouch and grinning from ear to ear. Tom stared in amazement as Bart emptied four pennies into his hand. 'Now how about that for Christmas generosity, eh?' said Bart, his eyes shining. 'He told me to share it wiv you. He might be too lazy to 'elp us but at least he takes pity on the poor.'

Chapter 15

A Purse for the Journey

At Micklow Manor, Baron Godric de Mordon struggled into the saddle of his stallion, his fat jowls quaking with indignation. *So the saucy wench had given him the slip had she? Jilted for a whey-faced novice who had scarce begun to shave! Well, Sir Ranulf could look elsewhere for a husband for his granddaughter.* If *she ever returned . . .*

Sir Ranulf de Lacy stood on the snowy steps of his home, his hunting hawk on his shoulder and his eyes as doleful as the bloodhound at his side. It was a damned uncomfortable business. After all, Baron Godric was a neighbour, with lands adjoining his own.

'You must come over for some hunting when the snows clear, Godric,' called Sir Ranulf as the baron's mount leapt ahead at a sharp jab from his spurs. 'Winter's the best time. Hare, boar, stag . . .' he tailed off as Baron Godric lurched away in a jangle of horse brass without a word of farewell.

Sir Ranulf puffed out his battle-scarred cheeks. The baron put him in mind of a Christmas pudding – pent up with furious steam and in danger of bursting its skin. He turned glumly from the open door. A merry Christmas Day this was turning out to be. It seemed Sir Ranulf's granddaughter had run off with a renegade novice. Baron Godric was mightily offended! And to make matters worse, his daughter Alice was even now waiting in the great hall with the miller, anxious for his advice as to what was to be done. As he strode down the hall to meet them, his bloodhound trotting mournfully at his heels, Sir Ranulf heaved a deep sigh. He blamed himself in no small measure for the business. Yet he had meant the betrothal for the best. The elderly baron had seemed so keen and with any luck he might only have lived a few years!

Alice Miller, one time de Lacy, stood in the grand hall of Micklow Manor, white faced and exhausted, twisting the empty honey jar in her hands. The festive garlands over the fireplace seemed to mock her grief. It was all her fault! A miller had been good enough for her, so why had she wanted fine cushions and beds with silk curtains for Bessie? Alice saw it clearly now; the folly of forcing a betrothal on a headstrong girl like Bessie. And now she might never see her again.

But Gabriel Miller, tight-lipped next to his wife, did not blame himself. He blamed Tom Fletcher with the righteous indignation of a father, keen to protect his daughter's honour. 'I am convinced Bessie is making for London,' he said, as Sir Ranulf drew near. 'You heard what they said at the abbey about the note from Bessie they found under the runaway's bolster. And yet I feel sure the scheme was his idea. The novice master tells me he is a most unruly troublemaker. The donkey's head outside the sacristy is certain proof that he stole from the abbey. The rogue must have attacked the abbot and left him for dead, escaping with the treasure!'

'But Gabriel,' said Alice tearfully. 'How can you know this for sure? Brother Thomas is not unknown to us. He is an unruly boy, I agree, and one not inclined for the life of a monk but this is attempted murder! It is a hanging offence!' And with that she burst into tears. 'Oh how I wish I had never heard of Baron Godric and then none of this would have happened!'

'Hush Alice, hush,' soothed Gabriel, placing his work-roughened hand on hers. 'Pray do not blame yourself. Bessie was led astray by that ruffian, Tom Fletcher. But this scandal will ruin her marriage prospects if they are not done for already.' He turned to Sir Ranulf, his voice full of pent up anger. 'They must be on foot since there are no horses missing from the abbey. I must go after them. I have wasted precious time already.'

'But Gabriel,' cried Alice, clutching his arm. 'You do not know London. You have never been further than ten miles from Saint Agnes Next-the-Sea. Oh Lord, I cannot bear it! There might be robbers, brigands . . . wolves!' she sobbed, turning as a sharp draft blew into the hall from the open curtain at her back. Fustian, Sir Ranulf's clerk, stepped into the firelight, dressed in new riding boots and swathed to his shaggy brows in a thick muffler. He coughed apologetically.

'I think you are forgetting something,' he said humbly, with a courteous bow in the miller's direction. 'Master Miller might be a stranger to London, but I most certainly am not. Do not forget I was clerk to Sir Percy FitzNigel for fifteen miserable years. I know every nook and cranny of that godforsaken city. If anyone can find your daughter in that stinking rat-hole . . . it is I.'

Sir Ranulf de Lacy stared at Fustian, a look of admiration on his face. 'God's bones! Well said, Fustian!' he cried in a hearty voice that set his hunting hawk a-flutter. 'You put me to shame. I cannot allow my clerk to outdo me in chivalry. I will come too and provide a purse for the journey as well! We will saddle our fastest steeds. God willing we will overtake them on the way. Let us pray this brutal weather keeps up. If there is a thaw the road to London will be a river of mud.'

Gabriel Miller was visibly moved and not a little relieved at the offer of company. 'I am grateful, Sir Ranulf,' he said. Then turning to his wife he took her sorrowful face in his hands. 'We will all go after Bessie, my dear. And you have my word of honour. We will find the villain, Tom Fletcher, and by all that is holy, we will bring our daughter safely home.'

Alone in her cold prison, Bessie had never felt more desolate in her life. At times she thought she heard footsteps, moving around on the floor above, but when she cried out for help, no one answered her call. She didn't know what to think. Her mind lurched between fury that Tom had deserted her, and desperation about what might have happened to him.

She was sure they hadn't discovered his hiding place – at least not before Sir Jocelyn had marched her off the boat. So why hadn't he come to rescue her?

Still, she refused to give up hope.

Perhaps he'd followed her and knew where she was and was even now going to fetch help. She had to believe it! But now as she groped forlornly around the damp walls of her prison, her imagination crawled with all the slimy deep-down things of nightmares; bats, spiders, toads . . . *rats!* The scream she had been fighting down now rose from her stomach to her chest and from her chest to her throat as she heard in the blackness the scuttle of running feet and the distinctive squeak she knew so well. How could a miller's daughter mistake the sound of rats?

Chapter 16

Water Quintain

'I'm a Bridge-Dweller. That's what they call us what
live on the bridge,' Bart told Tom proudly as he led
the way to his lodgings. He had to shout to make
himself heard over the whoosh of the thundering River
Thames. 'We can buy some larks' tongues on sticks wiv
the money what that Justice gave us – unless you'd prefer
an 'ot pie.'

A double row of tall shops and houses lined London
Bridge, some four, even five storeys high. They met
across the top to form a long torch-lit tunnel of furriers,
weavers, skinners and candle shops, extending behind on
stonework piles hanging precariously over the surging
river on massive wooden struts. Tom was hardly listening
to Bart, his mind a confusion of half-formed plans
about discovering who Balthazar was. There must be some
way of finding out – quickly before Sir Jocelyn shipped
Bessie off to Marrakech! Tom had been comforting

himself with the thought that if they meant to sell her as a slave they'd keep her safe – and healthy. But for how long?

'I need to plan what to do next,' shouted Tom, above the deafening noise.

'Can't hear you,' Bart shouted back, curling his hand round his ear. 'Say that again!'

'I need to make a plan to find Bessie!' yelled Tom.

Bart tapped his ear and screwed up his face. Tom threw up his hands in frustration. The noise was too loud to hear anything.

'I live between the rope maker's and the pastry shop,' called Bart over his shoulder. 'Keep up slow worm! You're an easy mark for a cut-purse! And I should know,' he added with a wink. Tom scurried up, closing the gap between them.

London Bridge was a fearful place, the shops so topsy-turvy that Tom was almost afraid to walk under the eaves for fear they'd collapse. Arches of strong timber linked the tops of the houses overhead, to keep them together and prevent them falling into the river. The bridge seethed with livestock, pigs, geese and carts. Tom had no choice but to tag along behind Bart with Flea at his side, weaving through the press of bodies and stepping around a shabby bear dancing forlornly to a tune played on a reed pipe.

Tom glanced nervously over his shoulder. He felt overwhelmed with anxiety but something else was bothering him too. It had started with a shiver down his spine but now it was stronger, more like a thousand flea bites on his back. When it had begun Tom couldn't rightly say, but for some time now he had sensed he was being followed. No one ever seemed to be looking in his direction however quickly he turned. But all the same, he felt eyes boring into his back.

It was dark on the bridge, reeking of smoke and wet straw, and yet the houses were hung with festive banners for the holiday and there were at least two cock fights well under way in a space hardly twelve feet wide. To Tom's relief, it was a little quieter in the tunnel-like street, although they could still hear the river and feel its vibrations, churning under their feet.

'I say, Bart. Do you know anyone I can ask about Balthazar?'

Bart frowned at Tom, his thick eyebrows meeting in the middle. And then he smiled his broken-toothed smile. 'We can ask me Pa when we get to my place. He knows everyone. He used to be Lord Mayor of London . . . a fair few years ago that is!'

Tom didn't believe him, but still his hopes soared. Bart seemed to know a lot of people so maybe his father, whoever he really was, did too. 'Let's go straight there then,' he said.

Suddenly a great roar went up from further down the bridge and to Tom's dismay, everyone started racing towards a gap in the houses, including Bart.

'Come on!' shouted Bart, doubling back and dragging Tom by the arm. 'There's a game of Water Quintain. We'll miss it if we're not quick! Let's see if we can find a place at the front.'

With Tom following reluctantly on his heels, Bart barged

through the crowd, elbowing a passage to the edge of the bridge. 'Now lean right over and watch them boats. They're gonna shoot the bridge. There's always a few people drowned!'

Tom peered over the edge of the parapet, his heart in his mouth. He'd never seen anything so terrifying. The bridge had nineteen arches, no two widths the same. The pillars or 'starlings' as Bart told him they were called, created little weirs, impeding the flow of the river. The tide was running out and the water plunged through the gaps at such tremendous speed the booming noise was deafening.

Bart laughed at the look on Tom's face. 'People actually row under it?' gasped Tom.

'Yeah. It's called "Shooting the Bridge". There's a saying. "Wise men walk over London Bridge while only fools go under it!" It's the most dangerous game in London. Look out!' shouted Bart. 'It's starting!'

West of the bridge some men had fixed a great tree trunk in the middle of the river, bearing two targets. Tom watched in amazement as a score of little rowing boats gathered further upstream. Each boat had two oarsmen and in each stern stood a waterman, holding a huge lance.

Bart's eyes were shining with excitement. 'The tide has turned, see. It's runnin' out under the bridge. When the ship's trumpet sounds, the oarsmen row as fast as they can downstream with the tide. The watermen have to hit the target and break their lance. If the lance don't snap they fall into the river. You'll hear them screaming for their lives! Lots get swept clean away!'

* * *

Bart had enjoyed the sport hugely, although he seemed downcast that nobody had drowned. 'That was quite a good shoot but I've seen better!' said Bart. 'There are fifty men drowned every year shootin' the bridge. And that's ones that know what they're doing! Me father used to be a champion Quintain player . . . until he got his gammy leg.'

The crowds were dispersing now. Bart squinted up at the watery sun. 'Oops. I nearly forgot! Flea's got a job today,' he said. 'He's appearin' at *The Three Cripples* at the end of the bridge. We'd best be cutting along.'

'Hey! Don't forget you said we'd go to your place,' reminded Tom anxiously. 'You promised we'd ask your father if he knew anybody called Balthazar . . .'

'All right! All right!' said Bart irritably. 'We'll drop in at me lodgings on our way to the inn.'

But to Tom's disappointment there was no one at home when Bart popped his head round his door. 'Don't look so worried!' said Bart with a grin. 'Me Pa will be in *The Three Cripples* already, I'll wager. I'll introduce you just as soon as Flea's done 'is turn.'

Tom clenched his teeth. Bart was impossible and yet there was no one else he felt he could ask.

The Three Cripples Inn was even dirtier than *The Dog's Head*. It clung to the river bank at the northern end of the bridge, its walls covered in weed and slime. Old rags hung at the low windows and the earth walls dripped with moisture from the fug of stale breath and the steam from the wassail bowl seething on the fire. Everyone seemed to know everybody else and it was clear that Bart and Flea were expected. *Flea's got a job*, Bart had said. *What can he have meant?*

'Is your father here, Bart?' asked Tom as soon as they ducked under the lintel. He peered into the gloom, looking for features that resembled Bart's. Bart squinted into the shadows. 'Can't see 'im yet,' he replied with a shrug. 'He's probably on 'is way now.'

Tom bit his lip. This was the second wild goose chase he'd been on with Bart, and he was still no nearer finding Bessie. He felt out of place here, his face growing hot under the curious stares of the bridge-dwellers with their wolfish dogs. Maybe this accounted for the growing feeling of unease; the sensation of eyes on the back of his jerkin. He glanced furtively over his shoulder but no one had come in after them through the smoke-blackened door.

At one end of the ramshackle room was a small stage with two rows of half-barrels forming a semi-circular ring of seats. A jester with a cap of bells had just tumbled from the stage in a roar of hoots and stamping feet into the arms of a tavern wench.

'Follow me and grab one of them free stools on the back row,' said Bart as he elbowed his way through the surge of applause. 'Here's me cap. When Flea's finished 'is turn you can hand it round. Wiv any luck it'll pay for our supper.'

Tom slumped down on a half-barrel with a scowl, jiggling his knees with impatience. Supper was the last thing on his mind. However, Bart's singing took him by surprise.

It was pure and golden, and smooth as liquid honey, and as Bart sang a mournful song of lost love, Flea raised himself on his square haunches and crooned along with his master, his whiskers a-quiver with feeling. Tom could almost imagine a tear in Flea's eye. He glanced uneasily over his shoulder towards the door. There was nobody behind him. Perhaps it was Bart's golden voice that was sending those shivers down his spine.

All of a sudden there was a change of mood. Tom turned back towards the stage. The spectators held their breath whilst Bart fished a tin whistle from his cat-skin jerkin and began a rollicking jig, as merry and wild as the last song had been sad. In perfect time with the jig, Flea began to dance, around and around on his two hind legs, his mouth wide and panting and his huge tongue lolling with the effort. The audience clapped and stamped in time, a rhythmic accompaniment of hands and feet and the faster they drummed their feet, the faster Bart's fingers danced up and down the whistle. Flea was a whirlwind of feet and fur as the audience rose up in a standing ovation.

As the people surged forward towards the stage in a burst of thunderous appreciation, Tom remembered the cap to collect the money for dinner. Amidst the whoops and whistles, he leaned forward and began to grope for the cap which had fallen onto the ale-sodden sawdust. He bent over and stared between his knees. He had no sense of the shadowy form creeping up behind him; no sense of imminent danger. He was still feeling for the missing cap when the barrel was kicked from under him and he felt the sting of cold steel in the place where his jerkin ended and his stolen breeches began.

The blade had drawn blood, the pain like a shiver of cold

fire but Tom had no time to think of that or the ache in his knees where he'd hit the floor. The gag they had stuffed between his teeth had forced his tongue back towards his windpipe so he could hardly draw breath let alone swallow. A sack was pulled roughly over his head from behind. No one came to his aid. Everyone was so caught up with the dancing dog that no one had seen it happen – or if they had, nobody cared. Now his attackers were binding his hands. Then, with the applause from the crowd still ringing in his ears, Tom was bundled outside and hefted clumsily into a cart, banging his head hard on the wooden planking as he fell. He heard his captors cursing as they pulled a tarpaulin over him and roped it down.

With a sudden lurch the cart was off, jolting along the street, rattling through winding alleys, the clamour of church bells chiming the hour.

Perhaps these were the cut-purses Bart had mentioned! thought Tom. When they found he hadn't a penny, maybe they'd let him go. But then again . . . maybe they'd slit his throat!

Panic coursed through Tom's body as he juddered along like a carcass to market, and with every jerk over the rough cobbles he heard the voice of Abbot Fergus in his ears. '*London's a fearful place! London's a fearful place!*'

Chapter 17

Three Golden Crowns

As Tom Fletcher clattered through the mean, dirty streets of the city, Gabriel Miller and his companions trotted despondently under the wide stone arch of *The Pious Pilgrim Inn*, half-way between Saint Agnes and London. A child with a face like a ferret came scurrying over the yard in a pool of yellow lantern light to take the horses' reins.

'We will take meat and drink for the journey, Master Miller,' said Sir Ranulf dismounting. 'And who knows? Perhaps we will hear news of Bessie.'

Gabriel Miller grunted as he swung his right leg across his mare's wide back and dropped down into the snow. 'I have prayed for tidings every step of the way, at every dismal hamlet we have ridden through, but still no sign of Bessie. Perhaps they did not travel this road after all . . . or maybe we have overtaken them without knowing it . . .'

'Do not torture yourself, Master Miller,' said Fustian,

handing his horse to the stable boy. 'You have done all that a father possibly could. You have searched every hedgerow and ditch yourself.'

'Welcome travellers, welcome!' cried the eager landlord, hurrying across the yard in a pair of sagging britches, his rabbit-skin cap pulled down tight against the cold. This was good fortune indeed. All inns were short of business in December. He snatched off his cap and scraped a bow towards Sir Ranulf. Fustian shrank into the shadow of his hood, hoping the landlord wouldn't remember him from when he'd worked for Sir Percy.

As if reading the humble clerk's thoughts, the landlord stopped suddenly in his tracks. His smile froze, his welcoming face transformed by a scowl. 'But don't I know you?' he asked, thrusting a lantern in Fustian's face. 'By God, I do! You're the servant of that wretched King's Justice that ate all my victuals and rode off without paying!'

Fustian cleared his throat and returned the landlord's bow. 'Pray forgive me, Landlord. I *was* once his clerk, such was my misfortune. But now I serve Sir Ranulf de Lacy,' he said, proudly, straightening up and pulling back his shoulders, 'at a wage of four pence a day!'

Sir Ranulf placed a protective arm around Fustian's narrow back. 'Come landlord, enough of this,' he said jovially. 'It was hardly this poor devil's fault if he worked for a Justice that didn't pay his way. But you may rest assured I've a purse for the journey, and Sir Ranulf de Lacy *never* leaves without paying his dues!' And with that he steered Fustian before him across the yard and into the fuggy warmth of the wayside inn, the miller following dejectedly behind.

But there was no news of the fugitives at *The Pious Pilgrim*. Scarcely a visitor, lamented the landlord, let alone a pilgrim. So, in the smoky parlour hung with dried savoury and thyme, Gabriel Miller was all for retracing their steps. *They had passed Bessie on the way, he was sure of it. Perhaps there was another road to London Sir Ranulf did not know? Bessie's boots were not stout; the soles were too thin; her cloak was too threadbare.* And so he fretted, whilst the landlord served mutton stew from a cauldron above the fire and Sir Ranulf ordered an earthenware jug of spiced wine.

'They could still be ahead of us on the road,' Sir Ranulf reasoned, seating himself by the fire with his stale bread trencher of stew. 'After all, we think they left Saint Agnes last night. You told me yourself that your daughter's bed had not been slept in. *We* did not set out until this morning and then not until the sun was well up. The way ahead is clear. If we do not overtake them on the road to London, when we reach the city we will go directly to the sheriff and seek his aid. I will ask him to issue a description of that rogue, Tom Fletcher, and a warrant for his arrest.'

Gabriel nodded grimly. Everyone meant to be kind and he was grateful for the company on the lonely road but his heart was as heavy as the iron kettle that steamed on the hearth. Sir Ranulf had better be right. For how could he return to Saint Agnes Next-the-Sea and face his poor wife unless Bessie was riding behind him?

* * *

It was dark in the in which cellar they had flung Tom, yet not so dark that he couldn't see. There was no light around the edge of his prison door and not even a keyhole, but a few faint beams of moonlight shone in from a grating high up in the opposite wall. At last, when Tom's hands were raw with beating against the iron-studded door, he leaned his forehead against it, stamping his foot in rage.

Something hard crunched under his boot, the smallest sensation as if he'd stepped on a pea. He looked down without interest, miserably lifting his foot to examine the sole of his boot. It was a scarlet berry, now squashed flat with his weight. He flicked it off onto the floor and it was then that he noticed the ribbon – a thin yellow coil at the edge of a pool of moonlight. He picked it up. It was a necklace strung with berries but the ribbon had snapped and some of the fruit was scattered on the floor. It looked like a charm ribbon, similar to the ones that Bessie was always weaving. He swallowed. As if he needed reminding of Bessie!

Tom narrowed his eyes and sniffed. What was that smell? Something riverish; dank, rotten and slightly fishy. And now he realised why. The cellar was full of puddles of river water and he could hear the rushing of the River Thames outside. He must be in the cellar of a building on the bank of the river – and a leaky one at that. And to make matters worse, he was not alone. With a shudder of disgust, he felt something brush against his ankle and he heard the squeak of rats.

Tom groped for his dagger. *At least there'd been one stroke of luck in an ill-fated day*, he thought, fingering the device of the three crowns carved into the dagger's hilt. And then something struck him like a bolt of lightning!

He had only caught a fleeting glimpse of the strangers as they'd loosed his hands and thrust him into the cellar. But something distinctive had caught Tom's eye and now he realised what it was. His attackers had worn woollen cloaks, caught up at the shoulder with a decorative metal clasp. Nothing unusual in that, except that the design on the clasp was the same as the one on the hilt of his dagger!

Three golden crowns!

Tom felt a curious falling sensation, as if he'd jumped over a low wall and found the drop on the other side was longer than he'd guessed. Three crowns on the flag he'd found on board *Los Tres Magos*, three crowns on the dagger . . . and now three crowns on the clasps of his captors' cloaks!

The device was everywhere! Three crowns must be Sir Jocelyn's coat of arms so that made his attackers Sir Jocelyn's men! And that meant his capture *was* connected with Bessie! These were no hit and miss villains. They'd been after *him*. Not just anybody but *him*, Tom Fletcher!

And yet none of it made sense. He was convinced no one had seen him on the ship. He'd remained hidden until he'd woken to the sound of church bells. No one but Bessie and Bart knew he was in London. So if no one had seen him aboard the boat, how could anyone come looking for him? But come looking they certainly had!

Tom's flesh began to prickle, not simply with fear, but with a curious feeling of excitement. His situation was desperate. And yet some small germ of hope was growing. He opened his hand and peered once again at the charm ribbon. A shiver ran down his spine. *If these were the same people who had taken Bessie, then maybe she was somewhere nearby. Was the ribbon* similar *to the ones Bessie made – or was it actually hers?*

As his eyes adjusted to the gloom, Tom began to grope around the damp walls of his prison, feeling along the rough stones for any signs of an opening; any possible means of escape. If Bessie was near, he had to get out and rescue her.

The cellar was a kind of storeroom. A pyramid of barrels was stacked at one end, and in the corner there was a circular iron grating which seemed to cover the entrance to a drain. *That explains the water! And the rats!* thought Tom, with a grimace. How useful. A waterside cellar. Perfect for a smugglers' den.

Looking up, Tom saw huge lumpy shapes hanging from iron hooks in the beams of the ceiling. He almost cried out in fright, and then he laughed with relief. What he'd thought were bodies were just great bales of fur pelts and animal skins. He narrowed his eyes and reached up to push the pelts aside, peering between the rafters. A rectangle of light glowed in the centre of the ceiling – the outline of a trapdoor. Suddenly the rafters creaked and Tom heard a door bang. He held his breath. Someone was moving about on the floorboards overhead. Then he heard muffled voices and the scrape of a chair.

Tom strained his ears.

'G . . . good evening, sir,' stammered a tremulous voice from above. 'Have you brought the package? My master said to be sure to ask for it if you called whilst he was out.'

'Did he, by Jove! And pray tell me. What sort of a package is he expecting?'

Tom gave a violent start. It was Jocelyn de Maltby's voice, he could swear it! But who was his companion? A servant perhaps – but not Sir Jocelyn's it seemed.

'I wouldn't know, Sir Jocelyn,' replied the first voice. 'My master told me you'd know what he was talking about.'

Sir Jocelyn gave a scornful laugh. 'I know what he's talking about all right. So typical of Balthazar! He never could get his priorities right. Well, you can tell him he'll have to wait until tomorrow. Haven't I done enough for one day? I've dealt with that stowaway girl I found on *Los Tres Magos* and the wretched boy too. And now I must bid you good night. I only came with a message for Balthazar. Tell him I've arranged the girl's passage to Marrakech – for the day after tomorrow, at the turn of the tide.' Tom stifled a gasp. 'I've moved her to a secure place,' Sir Jocelyn laughed, 'to await the next stage of her journey.'

'Very good, Sir Jocelyn,' replied the servant. 'Good night.'

Tom heard the sound of retreating footsteps; the creak of a closing door. *So Sir Jocelyn was behind his capture!* he thought with a shiver of excitement. *This must be Balthazar's house, whoever Balthazar was. So where was Bessie? If she was waiting for a ship she was bound to be somewhere by the river.* He had to escape! He had to find her . . . before it was too late.

Gradually the candlelight from above began to dwindle. Tom imagined the mysterious servant snuffing out wicks one by one. He stared hopelessly at the pyramid of barrels stacked against the wall. Of course he could climb the barrels but they were too far away from the trapdoor in the centre of the cellar. If only he could drag some of the kegs into the middle.

It wouldn't be easy. One keg was not tall enough and two might be too many. There would have to be enough room for him to crouch on the topmost cask. If there was, he could use the full strength of his arms to push upwards on the wooden trapdoor. He narrowed his eyes and assessed the dimensions of the barrels. It might just work . . .

Excitement made Tom hungry. He'd eaten nothing for hours and slept even less. He wondered if Bessie was hungry too. *And what must Bart be thinking? Had Flea earned enough to pay for their dinner? Bart must think him ungrateful – running off without even waiting for supper.* He rolled up his sleeves and picked his way around the puddles to the barrels. He was thirsty too. Perhaps they were full of wine, although there was no way of getting at it. It seemed odd to be thirsty in a cellar full of drink.

The barrels were indeed full, much heavier than Tom had imagined, and his fingernails were soon torn and bloody with the effort of pulling and pushing. It was hard to get a grip on their curving sides and his hands were full of splinters. But at last he came up with a trick. If he heaved them over onto their sides, he discovered he could roll them more easily into position. Even so, every large keg took all his strength to move and then it was another exhausting task to drag them upright again. At last he had two barrels in place in the centre of the cellar. He turned his back and placed both hands behind him on the top of one of the kegs, heaving himself up so that he was sitting on its flat top. Then scrambling to his feet, he reached his hands above his head. At this level he could almost place the flat of his hands against the trapdoor but he was still not tall enough to push it open, even if he stood on tiptoe.

He sank to a crouch with a groan of disappointment. He needed to stack another barrel on the top but he simply didn't have the strength to lift it. It was hopeless. He sat on the barrel and kicked his heels in despair. Then drawing his knees to his chin, he wrapped his arms around his legs and rested his aching head on his knees. The moon had risen, so that it no longer shone through the grating. It was almost pitch black in the cellar. Cold as he was, Tom's eyelids began to droop. *Perhaps it was the bang on the head that was making his so sleepy*, he thought, as the fatigue of the day washed over him like a thick black tide.

Chapter 18

Toxic Honey

The moon climbed the church steeples through the long deep night and then slid down the sky and still Tom slept the dreamless sleep of exhaustion. But as the sun rose, gilding the snowy spires of London with a rosy light, he began to dream. *He was in the water meadows beside the River Twist. Herbert was wading towards him through the shallows and Tom's heart leapt. But even as he rushed towards his friend, Herbert's form evaporated away and Tom was alone. He was wading too, not in the River Twist, but through a slimy cellar awash with filthy river water. He felt thirsty – and suddenly a small barrel came floating along beside him. He stooped down and pulled out a wooden bung and raising the cask to his lips he began to drink . . .*

Tom awoke with a start – stiff and sore. Where was he? It was still gloomy in the cellar but the morning sun streamed through the grating, dappling a small patch of grimy wall with light. Church bells were chiming. Eight . . . nine . . . ten. *Ten o'clock*! On the morning after Christmas day. He suddenly remembered where he was . . . and he knew what he had to do . . .

Each barrel was firmly sealed on the top with a wide wooden bung, too firmly wedged to extract with his fingers. With mounting excitement, Tom groped for his dagger. Then, his tongue between his teeth, he inserted the fine point of the knife between the bung and the surrounding wood and began to lever – first one side and then the other. The stopper was stuck fast with gummy black tar that stained Tom's hands and made his fingers stick together. Then suddenly he heard a sharp hiss, followed by a splutter of ruby liquid and the sharp fruity smell of wine. A little more wiggling and he held the enormous bung in his hand. Then, bending low where the belly of the barrel began to taper down, he heaved with all his might.

The barrel tipped promisingly and then rocked back. Tom heaved again with a mighty groan of effort and over it toppled, the wine pumping out like blood from a wound. Tom cupped his hands and drank. The wine was icy cold and stung the back of his throat with its bitter oaky taste.

After what seemed an eternity, the torrent of wine became a stream and the stream a trickle until with very little effort, Tom rolled the barrel across the floor. Stretching his arms wide, he bent down and hugged it to his chest, his hands on either side of its flat ends. It was still heavy but at least he could lift it and after a deal of struggling he had it in position on the top of the two lower kegs, forming a small pyramid of three. Then using one of the lower barrels as a step up, he clambered onto the top. There was only just room for him to crouch beneath the rafters, his shoulders roughly scraping the beams. He listened intently, trying to steady his breathing.

There was no sound from the room above and yet how could he be sure nobody was there? He could feel his heart, thumping in his throat. *Come on Tom*, he told himself firmly. *What choice is there? You haven't made all this effort to lose your nerve now.* So with cold sweat trickling down his neck, he placed his hands flat on the underside of the trapdoor and heaved firmly upwards. It opened easily in a flood of morning sunlight. Tom's heart fluttered in his chest like a caged bird as he rose from a crouch and stepped up cautiously into the room above. He almost fainted with relief. He was quite alone.

Tom stood in the grand hall of a sumptuous house, blinking in the light that spilled from four large windows. A great fire blazed at one end of the hall under a huge stone chimney on which was carved the now familiar emblem of three crowns picked out in gold. There was clean, fragrant straw on the floor and the walls were hung with linen panels decorated with fine embroidery. This mysterious Balthazar must be rich indeed! There was a long trestle table in the centre of the room with polished benches on either side set with a broad damask cloth and dishes of wafers to dip in spiced wine. A jewelled jug and some goblets stood at one end in front of a large wooden dresser stacked with trenchers of gleaming silver.

Tom shivered. He'd been so intent on escaping he hadn't

had time to think what he'd do afterwards. If Bessie was somewhere nearby, he needed to find her quickly, before anyone discovered he'd escaped. He leaned down and swung the trap door back into place, scattering straw over the top. Then, with a wary glance up and down the hall, he tiptoed swiftly towards the door. At the end of the hall, near to the door, was another large trestle piled with books and rolls of parchment, an oil lamp hanging low on chains fixed to a broad oak beam.

At the side of the table stood a huge strong box with a large black lock and next to it, a tall iron sconce, bristling with candles, their wax frozen in all stages of lopsided melting. A pile of fresh yellow parchment lay on the table next to a pot of assorted quills and a large rectangular dish full of a brownish oily liquid, a piece of parchment in the bottom weighed down by a stone. Tom breathed in the familiar smell. Dust, oil and brine mixed together; an easy way to make parchment look old. And what was this next to it? Tom's eyes widened. A dish of assorted seals and ribbons, the kind used for important documents. A forger's paradise!

Tom glanced anxiously towards the door. All was silent. There was a small leather-bound book in the centre of the desk with a marker in it next to a half finished letter, a goose feather quill lying askew across the writing. Tom picked up the book carefully. His fingers were covered in sticky black tar from the bung. It wouldn't do to leave a tell-tale mark. He opened it at the owner's chosen place. *Toxic Honey*, he read. His mouth dropped open as he scanned the page. *Honey derived from bees fed solely on poisonous plants can have a strong toxic effect. Plants such as wormwood, rhubarb, aconite and hemlock are extremely effective. The bees remain unharmed.* Tom hurriedly closed the book, replacing it exactly where he had found it. And then he picked up the letter. *Dear Sir Henry*, he read, beneath the central design of three crowns. *I hope this small gift from my garden finds you much improved* . . . Cautiously, Tom picked up a small jar, wrapped in creamy parchment. The writing was the same as on the letter: *English Honey.*

Tom was shaking. This Balthazar was not only a murderer but a forger of documents and a dabbler in poisons too! How he'd known where to find Tom or even of Tom's existence was a puzzle he couldn't work out, but one thing was clear. Bessie was in grave danger. He had to find her! He cast his eyes rapidly over the desk as if willing it to yield up some clue. But there was nothing else except a large open book, the writing neat and regular. Tom read the title at the top of the page in Latin. *Treatise de legibus angliae.* 'On the laws of England,' he translated with a frown.

Tom looked up with a start. Someone was coming! He'd been so absorbed in examining the desk that he'd forgotten to listen out and now footsteps were approaching the door. He heard the jangle of keys. His heart skipped several beats. For a second Tom stood paralysed with fear and then with a gasp of panic he flung himself down by the strong box and heaved on the lid with all his strength. It wasn't locked but it was stiff. He heard the grate of a key in the hall door; the clattering of the latch, iron against iron. And at just that moment, the lid of the chest swung open with a creak.

In another second Tom was inside, pushing aside rolls of parchment and a pair of old leather boots. Crouching low, he lowered the lid over his head. He was just in time.

From the narrow gap between the edge of the lid and the side of the chest, Tom watched in terror as the double doors swung open. A tall figure in a travelling cloak entered with a graceful hound at his heels, stamping his snowy boots, his face aglow with cold. Pulling off his fur trimmed gloves, he strode purposefully towards the central table and poured a generous goblet of wine from the jewelled jug. Then turning on his heel, he walked back towards the door.

Tom clenched his jaw to stop himself from crying out. The man's hair was the colour of ripe corn, long to his clean-shaven jaw beneath a cap of soft wool. He pulled off his cloak and flung it over the desk. His long-sleeved tunic was lined with fur and over it he wore a sleeveless surcoat, embroidered with three golden crowns.

Sir Percy FitzNigel! Tom would have recognized those cruel green eyes anywhere!

Tom's heart almost stopped! The device of the three crowns had turned up yet again. He'd seen it three times in the space of a few minutes. Once above the fireplace in this grand hall and then on top of the letter lying on the desk . . . and *now* on the fine blue wool of Sir Percy FitzNigel's surcoat! *What was* he *doing here*? Tom's mind was racing. *Was the coat of arms Sir Percy's*? *And if it was, could this be Sir Percy's house*? He bit his lip. *So who was Balthazar*? He thought of the flag and the dagger. *Was the ship, Los Tres Magos, Sir Percy's too*?

Tom swallowed hard, remembering Sir Jocelyn's visit of the night before. The servant had said his master was expecting Sir Jocelyn to bring a package. *Was the servant's master none other than Sir Percy FitzNigel? And could the awaited package be the golden casket?* Tom's stomach turned over. *Perhaps Sir Percy FitzNigel was in league with Sir Jocelyn! But it couldn't be true! The King's Justice in league with the man with the silver finger!*

Sir Ranulf de Lacy's party had ridden through the night, so that as Tom had awoken to the chime of church bells in his damp cellar, the visitors from Saint Agnes were trotting under London Wall at Aldgate into the clamour of the city. Gabriel Miller's country horse tossed its head, shying at the unfamiliar sights and sounds. *So this was what Bessie had exchanged for Saint Agnes Next-the-Sea*, thought the miller bitterly, trotting along behind Sir Ranulf, his hand on his purse. *A godforsaken city and the company of a scoundrel! Although to be fair, she could never have known what London would be like.*

From London Wall, Sir Ranulf took charge, deftly evading the ragged beggars who clutched at his bridle and the hot-pie sellers who blocked his path crying their wares. Sir Ranulf knew London well from the days of his youth, when the glitter of the King's Court had seemed preferable to sleepy Micklow Manor. Yet now, as he trotted through the warren of cramped alleys with their rubbish-filled ditches and the stench of night-soil in his nostrils, he wondered at his own youthful folly.

Dismounting in Fish Street Hill, they tied their horses to a rail and asked the way to the sheriff's house. The sheriff was out of London until tomorrow, they were told. They asked after some lodgings. 'Lodgings at Christmas!' came the churlish reply. 'All of the inns is full!' However, the landlord of *The Mule* down the road had one last room and stabling to spare, so Sir Ranulf secured it with four pennies and a promise to return.

'It is too bad the sheriff is out of town today, but no matter,' said Sir Ranulf encouragingly. 'We will visit my old friend the Lord Chief Justice in Westminster. He can advise us how to proceed. I missed him at the autumn assizes when they sent that prancing peacock, Percy FitzNigel, in his stead. Although I shouldn't complain,' he added with a wink at Fustian. 'After all, I did manage to pinch his clerk from under his nose!'

'I've no regrets at leaving his service,' said Fustian, shaking his head. 'I never could abide FitzNigel for all that I worked for him for so many years. You did me a favour in taking me on.'

Gabriel Miller cleared his throat. 'If it's all the same to you, Sir Ranulf,' he said respectfully. 'I would prefer to stay within the city walls and make enquiries from door to door. After all, Bessie's note said she planned to make for London, and if there's any news to be had hereabouts, I want to be the first to know it. Pray take Fustian and ride on without me. I have already described Tom Fletcher to you, so you can provide the Lord Chief Justice with the necessary description.'

Sir Ranulf nodded his agreement. The miller would be

far better engaged in some active pursuit, he felt sure, and they would all meet up again in a few hours time.

It was a short ride across the city from east to west and soon Sir Ranulf and Fustian were passing under the wall through Ludgate, over the River Fleet and out of London into the Strand. 'That was tolerably fragrant for London,' called Sir Ranulf over his shoulder. 'This bitter weather freezes the midden heaps. Do you remember what the air used to be like here in summer, Fustian? So thick with flies you could barely see your nose in front of your face!'

They were following the river now, around the huge curve of the Thames as it flowed from Westminster. And as the great abbey came into view, the air began to smell sweeter, the tiled roofs of the grand palaces of the lords and bishops sparkling white in the sun.

It was many years now since Sir Ranulf had visited his old friend the Lord Chief Justice near Westminster Hall. So he was disappointed to learn from a servant that Sir Henry was too ill to be disturbed. Indeed he had not left his bed for a week and could not get up for anyone.

'Not even for his old friend Sir Ranulf de Lacy?'

The worried servant scurried off to ask again. Sir Henry sent his compliments, but truly, he was not fit to see anyone. Sir Ranulf passed a weary hand over his face. This was a game of hare and hounds and no mistake. Yet they had to do something to find Bessie. How could he face the miller back at *The Mule* with nothing to report?

Sir Ranulf looked meaningfully at Fustian, scratching his broad flat nose. 'Well, it goes against the grain and all my better instincts,' he said, 'but then we really have little choice . . .'

Fustian returned his look in alarm. 'You surely do not mean . . . ?'

'I heard Sir Percy FitzNigel was building a house in this district,' said Sir Ranulf with a nod. 'He was full of his plans at the autumn assizes.' He gazed up and down the bustling street, then hailed a passer by who was scurrying past with his hood pulled up. 'Ho! You there!' he beckoned. 'Over here! Could you point us the way to FitzNigel Hall?'

The stranger could indeed. Sir Percy's new house was well known, and within minutes, Sir Ranulf de Lacy was leading the way across the Justice's snowy courtyard.

'I tell you, you're wasting your time with Sir Percy, if you'll pardon me for saying so,' grumbled Fustian as he drooped behind Sir Ranulf, his linen coif tied under his chin. Fustian's shoulders had already begun to sag. 'I hoped I'd never clap eyes on that devil again.'

'Now, now, Fustian,' Sir Ranulf replied firmly. 'Enough of that! You have nothing to fear from him now. I will appeal to him as a gentleman. So shoulders squared, there's a good fellow! You've fine wool on your back and a wage of four pence a day.'

'*Gentleman*!' exploded Fustian. 'If he's a gentleman then I'm a . . .'

'Enough, Fustian!' Sir Ranulf silenced him with a frown. 'Whether you like the Justice or not is quite beside the point. At the moment we have need of his help.'

Chapter 19

The King's Seal

On the other side of the courtyard in the grand solar of FitzNigel Hall, Tom had a crick in his neck. *How long would he have to stay hidden?* To his dismay, the Justice had taken a seat at the desk. Tom could hear his goose feather quill scratching swiftly over the parchment. And to make matters worse, Sir Percy's greyhound had wandered over to his hiding place and was sniffing around the chest. Tom could see the gleam in its eyes and smell its doggy breath. '*Oh God*,' he prayed. '*Don't let the dog give me away.*'

'Settle down, Plato!' commanded Sir Percy irritably. 'You've had your morning exercise!' The dog whined, turned round twice and slumped down by the strongbox with a thud. The Justice tipped sand over the letter to dry the ink, then held the document at arm's length. 'To Sir Percy FitzNigel,' he murmured. 'The grant of the farm known as Mallow Field, Hog Lane *in perpetuity*,' he read, his lips peeling back from his horsy teeth in a wicked grin. *Mallow Field – mine forever*! he thought to himself with a smile. The rents and tithes from Mallow Farm would come in very handy for the new building works at FitzNigel Hall. *Where does all my money go*? he wondered, stroking the ermine trim of his surcoat. Now for the King's seal! He selected a large metal disk from the bowl on the desk. 'This is the fellow,' he said, peering closely at the device engraved in reverse on the metal. '*Henry III*.' He held a candle to a fat stub of sealing wax and watched the ruby fluid trickle thickly onto the ribbon that hung from the parchment, and then pressed home the seal with a fizz. 'A beautiful forgery, even though I say so myself!' he muttered. 'Now no one can dispute that it's mine!'

Sir Percy glanced impatiently at his water clock, dripping the minutes into a crystal bowl. Sir Jocelyn de Maltby was late and he had a bone to pick with him. Well, a few bones if truth be told. His silver-fingered friend had made a pretty mess of the business with the casket – and a dangerous one too. He looked anxiously towards the door and then impatiently at the dog by the side of his desk. Plato was on his feet again, circling the strong box and scratching at the straw around it. Tom closed his eyes, trying not to meet the dog's gleaming gaze.

There was a sudden sharp knock on the door. To Tom's huge relief, the greyhound leapt to the threshold and began to bark. Sir Percy got up from his desk and strode down the hall, striking a pose with his back to the door. *This must be Sir Jocelyn now. This was a bad business and he was going to give his foxy friend a piece of his mind.* A moment later and his servant, Humphrey Pickerel, opened the door.

'You have some visitors, Sir Percy,' announced Pickerel. Tom recognized the voice at once. It was the servant he'd overheard talking with Sir Jocelyn last night.

'Show Sir Jocelyn in, Pilchard!' cried the King's Justice without turning round.

'It is not Sir Jocelyn, my Lord,' said Pickerel, bowing low. 'It is Sir Ranulf de Lacy of Saint Agnes Next-the-Sea. And his clerk Fustian.'

Tom couldn't believe his eyes. *Sir Ranulf de Lacy, the Lord of his Manor! Was he in league with them too*?

'Greetings of the season to you, Sir Percy!' boomed Sir Ranulf as he strode across the threshold. 'We have come to ask your help to find a renegade novice by the name of Thomas Fletcher, who has kidnapped my granddaughter and run off to London. The wretched boy is a thief and a scoundrel!'

Tom felt hot blood rush to his cheeks. *A thief and a scoundrel!* He shrank into himself, the blood pounding in his ears. *What was all this about?*

Sir Percy's green eyes narrowed in indignation. *What could Sir Ranulf be thinking of – barging uninvited into his home on Christmas day? And wasn't that Fustian, his frayed old clerk?*

'But gentlemen,' protested the Justice. 'It is still Christmas! A holiday. Is the King's Justice to have no peace from idle tittle-tattle? What, pray, has this to do with Sir Percy FitzNigel?'

A look of irritation clouded Sir Ranulf's brow. He had

never liked FitzNigel. But then again, they needed his help. 'This novice attacked the abbot of Saint Wilfred's Abbey, leaving him for dead!' announced Sir Ranulf. 'We also have reason to believe he has kidnapped my granddaughter and fled to London with a valuable relic stolen from the abbey. These are all hanging offences if I am not mistaken!'

Hanging offences! Fear seized Tom by the throat. His ears began to sing. If he'd been standing up he might well have fainted.

At the mention of the relic, Sir Percy's face twitched. His expression darkened like still water when the wind blows suddenly chill. And then all at once it changed swiftly, as if the sun had just come out.

'A novice did you say?' asked Sir Percy casually. *So now he understood who the boy was – and the girl for that matter. It was all beginning to make sense.* 'Pray forgive me for being over hasty. As King's Justice I am burdened down with trivial business but we are old friends are we not, Sir Ranulf? Your granddaughter did you say? Porpoise!' he rapped. 'Fetch our guests some spiced wine!'

But Humphrey Pickerel didn't seem to have heard. He was staring at the dog, which had returned to the chest and was prowling around it, hackles raised. *Oh God*! thought Tom. His eyes slid towards the desk where Sir Percy was leaning. *The evidence of forgery and poisoning was right there. If he was discovered in the chest, perhaps he could throw himself on Sir Ranulf's mercy and expose Sir Percy for a villain. But how would that help? It had nothing to do with the casket and Bessie – the crimes of which he was accused.*

Fortunately Sir Percy was too occupied with his visitors to notice the dog's antics. 'Pilchard,' he rapped again. 'I said bring some wine!' He flashed his teeth at Sir Ranulf. 'Pray sit down and tell me all. What does this novice look like? If it is in my power to help, I will assist you in any way that I can.'

Tom trembled as he listened to Sir Ranulf's tale – and not just with fear of discovery. He was gripped by a furious anger as he heard the accusations against him. *Abbot Fergus left for dead and he, Tom Fletcher, accused! Had he a reputation for stealing? No! For violence? No! And worst of all, did Abbot Fergus believe him capable of all this? And did Herbert think so too?* But as Sir Ranulf de Lacy told his tale, the evidence piling up against him, Tom started to see their point. The casket was missing and so was he. The donkey's head had been found by the sacristy window and he'd been the donkey. And everyone knew he wanted to leave Saint Wilfred's. He'd made no secret of that.

And as Tom listened, the King's Justice listened too, his cruel eyes aglitter with pleasure and surprise. He could hardly believe his luck. If he had been a praying man, he would have said these country visitors had brought the answer to his prayers.

Tom wondered what he should do? Should he leap out of the chest and tell Sir Ranulf what had really happened in Saint Agnes? But why would he believe him? *Sir Ranulf doesn't know me,* thought Tom. *I know him. Everybody knows the Lord of the Manor. But he doesn't know me! Sir Percy will deny all knowledge of everything. And why should Sir Ranulf believe an unknown novice over a King's Justice?* Then something else struck him. A thought that made Tom sick with fear. *If Sir Percy was in league with Sir Jocelyn, Sir Ranulf's accusations would suit them both very well. If they hanged him for a thief, he'd never be able to tell what he'd seen! No. To reveal himself to Sir Ranulf was a risk he dared not take. He had better stay hidden until the coast was clear and then try and find Bessie. She would speak up for him and clear his name! Showing himself now could be his death warrant!* Tom felt the bile rise in his throat. He had seen public hangings before.

Sir Percy FitzNigel was speaking now, his braying tone setting the glasses on the table ringing. 'You were absolutely right to come to me, since the sheriff is away and the Lord Chief Justice is ill,' he declared, his face all encouraging smiles. 'As I have told you, I will do everything in my power to bring this scoundrel to justice. I will issue a description of the vagabond and also of your granddaughter. I have my ways of investigating,' he continued with a conspiratorial wink. 'There is rarely a crime committed that Sir Percy FitzNigel does not uncover,' he boasted. 'Scarcely a misdemeanour occurs that goes unpunished!'

Sir Ranulf made an impatient sound in his throat. He was relieved that Sir Percy had agreed to help him but really the man was a pompous fool. It was too bad about dear old Sir Henry de Mandeville. He wondered what ailed him so badly that he could not even receive his old friend.

'We are obliged to you, Sir Percy,' said Sir Ranulf. 'And now I must hasten back to my lodgings. The girl's father has come to London with us and is even now making enquires in the city. If you have any information for us – we are all staying at *The Mule Inn* on Fish Street Hill.'

Tom's heart beat faster. *Bessie's father in London too! If only he'd come with Sir Ranulf! Maybe Gabriel Miller would have believed him. But he hadn't come – and it was too late now.* Sir Percy was already ushering Sir Ranulf towards the door. The Justice knew the tavern well and they could rest assured that any news he gathered would reach them there without fail.

'Of course,' concluded Sir Percy, 'when the villain is brought to trial, I will need you as witnesses to prove the case.' And with a reassuring smile, he ordered Pickerel to show them out. 'And put that restless dog in the yard whilst you're about it, Pilchard. I don't know what's wrong with him today.'

Fustian, bringing up the rear, made to scuttle past Sir Percy, hoping he wouldn't be noticed.

'You've done well for yourself, Fustian,' hissed Sir Percy, as Sir Ranulf de Lacy passed out of earshot. 'Much too well, I should say, for a clerk with so little talent!'

Fustian coughed behind his hand. 'No thanks to you,' mumbled the clerk.

'What was that Fustian?' replied Sir Percy, with a frown. He never had trusted this fellow.

'I said, "that's very true", Sir Percy,' Fustian replied, scurrying out through the grand door of FitzNigel Hall.

Sir Ranulf de Lacy was pleased to leave. There was something about the King's Justice he didn't trust. He lost no time in ushering his clerk down the sweeping stone steps and out into the frosty air. So he did not see the auburn-haired knight as he slipped from his hiding place behind the door and into the grand solar of FitzNigel Hall, the sun glinting on his silver finger.

Chapter 20

The Two Wise Men

Cramped in the chest, Tom was numb with shock. And to make matters worse he felt sure Sir Percy's servant had suspicions about his hiding place. He'd noticed him staring at the chest when the dog was snuffling around it. At least the young man had gone away for the moment, and taken that wretched hound with him. But Tom's reprieve was soon over. For the next minute, Humphrey Pickerel opened the door again and Sir Jocelyn de Maltby strode in. Sir Percy turned at the sound of the knight's leather boots on the rush-strewn floor. He sprang back in mock surprise, a theatrical hand to his chest.

'Ah, Melchior! So you have come at last!' Sir Percy's tone was sarcastic, his green eyes hard as emeralds. 'Porpoise!' he called to his servant. 'Stir your flippers and fetch Sir Jocelyn some wine!'

Humphrey Pickerel moved down the hall to the table set with wine cups, his jaw clenched in irritation. He poured a goblet of ruby wine for Sir Jocelyn, then swirling the jug to set the bitter dregs a-whirl, he poured a second for Sir Percy, praying he'd choke on the sediment. Then turning from the table he paused and stared down at the point in the floor where Tom had emerged through the trapdoor.

Tom's heart lurched. He'd hastily kicked the straw back in place when he'd climbed up into the room . . .but maybe not well enough.

'Hurry up, Pilchard!' rapped Sir Percy. 'What are you goggling at with those fishy eyes of yours?'

Humphrey Pickerel looked startled. 'Er . . . er nothing, Sir Percy. Only the merest splash of wine!'

Tom breathed again as he watched Pickerel tread slowly down the hall carrying the goblets on a silver tray. His mouth was dry with panic, but the servant merely handed the wine to the two men with a low bow and only the briefest glance at the chest where Tom was hiding.

'I trust you have the casket with you this time, Melchior!' said Sir Percy. 'Thus far you have only delivered a weeping girl and a scrawny boy.'

Sir Jocelyn fixed Sir Percy with a level gaze. Tom watched with bated breath as he reached within his cloak and removed a bag of knobbly leather from around his neck with a mocking smile. 'Of course I have the casket! What do you take me for, Balthazar?' he replied. 'A traitor like our friend Caspar?'

Balthazar! Tom sucked in his breath. Suddenly everything fell into place. Of course! Sir Percy FitzNigel and Balthazar were one and the same! He watched Sir Percy's eyes flick greedily over the package. The Justice was visibly relieved, yet still his tone was frosty. 'That was a careless incident aboard *Los Tres Magos*, Melchior,' he said, snatching the leather bag from Sir Jocelyn and locking it swiftly away in a cupboard. 'I hardly need to remind you that if you must use violence, it is better to do it in private. Especially someone with a distinctive mark like yours. Everyone knows The Man with the Silver Finger. Who knows what trouble those two young stowaways might have caused, had we not got them safely locked up?'

Sir Jocelyn de Maltby laughed. 'And who are *you* to speak of carelessness, Balthazar?' he said coldly, his hand on his sword. 'That's rich coming from you! It was a trifle 'careless' was it not, to strangle Caspar in a fit of rage – a murder much less easy to cover up than mine. Especially now – since his body has come to light at the foot of Dead Man's Stairs. You did not weigh him down with sufficient stones.'

'So typical of Caspar,' Tom heard Sir Percy snarl. 'To turn up when he's least wanted.'

'Nonetheless, it was a foolish loss of temper on your part, Balthazar, and one that may yet see us hang. The Abbot of Westminster is a powerful man. He will not let the murder of his sacrist go unpunished.'

'Caspar deserved all he got,' snapped Sir Percy. 'To betray The Three Wise Men – after all we have been through together. You were not there, Melchior. You do not know how the devil taunted me. He told me he had promised the casket to the Abbot of Westminster in return for favours for himself. And when I discovered he had sent the casket from London to prevent you from selling it and dividing the proceeds between us . . . well, as I say . . . he got what was coming to him.'

'I have always had more self-control than you, Balthazar,' replied Sir Jocelyn. 'I repeat. Your carelessness was greater than mine.'

For a moment they glared at one another in silence. Sir Percy was the first to drop his eyes to the floor. 'I only meant to frighten the wretch and force him to give it back,' he conceded. 'But when he came towards me swinging the knotted rope and threatened to expose our crimes and claim "benefit of clergy" if we implicated him, then I lost my temper, I admit. . .'

Tom caught his breath. *Of course! Balthazar, the murderer!* At last the pieces of the puzzle were beginning to slide into place. The murdered sacrist of Westminster had been called Brother Gideon and yet these men called him Caspar. And they called each other Melchior and Balthazar. Those names were well known to Tom; the three magi in the Bible! *Tres magi* was Latin for three kings. *Los Tres Magos* was almost the same. Three crowns for three kings. And their ship – *Los Tres Magos* – The Three Wise Men! Sir Jocelyn de Maltby strode to the table and poured more wine for himself. 'Come, Balthazar,' he said with a wolfish grin. 'I did not come to quarrel with you. We are both guilty of crimes for which we could hang! If word of this gets out you will never become Chief Justice and I for one do not relish the thought of a noose around my neck. Yet let us not despair. We still have the golden casket and there is more good news. I have a buyer for it, although the price is still not fixed.' He narrowed his eyes. 'What price the gift of a magus? But you may rest assured that you will have money enough to complete your house, and another ten palaces besides. Amusing, is it not?' he laughed. 'That the Three Wise Men should come by such a fitting treasure! So lift your goblet with me and drink to the *Two* Wise Men, for that is what we have now become. And let us plan what to do with the boy.'

Sir Percy raised his goblet. 'I have news for you too, Melchior. You saw my visitors leaving just now – the knight Sir Ranulf and his rag-bag companion?'

Sir Jocelyn nodded.

'They have come to London looking for the girl. It seems she is Sir Ranulf de Lacy's granddaughter. The boy, however, is a runaway novice from the abbey of Saint Wilfred's, accused of kidnapping the girl, attempted murder of his abbot and theft of the casket!'

Sir Jocelyn's eyes widened in delight. Sir Percy nodded smugly. 'I cannot believe our good fortune,' he said. 'The boy is a perfect scapegoat – the answer to our prayers. What more fitting excuse do I need to hang the boy? He is accused of three serious crimes. As the King's Justice, I will pass sentence myself and we will have no more to fear from his blabbing tongue. But we must dispose of the girl quickly, especially now her family has arrived.'

Sir Jocelyn frowned. 'Didn't Pickerel give you the message I left for you last night? She leaves tomorrow at the turn of the tide. A healthy Christian girl will fetch a handsome sum in the slave markets of Marrakech!'

Chapter 21

Silent feet

Humphrey Pickerel padded softly about the empty hall after Sir Jocelyn and Sir Percy had left, poking the fire and clearing the goblets of wine. Tom's nerves were stretched thin. His back ached and he could hardly bear the cramped position any longer. He was confused. *Did the servant really suspect he'd escaped from the cellar? Or had Tom imagined he was staring at the chest? Surely if he'd known he'd have raised the alarm.* There was a metallic taste in Tom's mouth. He'd been biting his lip so hard it was bleeding and his nails had made cuts in his palms.

Tom watched anxiously as the servant walked down the hall towards the door carrying the silver tray of dirty goblets. He stopped at the window staring thoughtfully out into the garden, then putting the tray down on the floor, he reached up and flung the window open wide. Tom felt a blast of freezing air slice in through the casement. The servant bent down again and picked up the tray. As he moved towards the door he paused by the chest where Tom was hiding. *This is it*! thought Tom, a cold sweat trickling down his spine. *Could he fight this servant and win*? Tom put his hand on his dagger. But to his immense surprise, Pickerel leaned down and cleared his throat softly. 'It is too bad,' muttered the servant, as if to himself. 'They have locked the girl in the boathouse – down by the water stairs.' Pickerel stared hard at the gap between the rim of the chest and its lid. 'The window to the garden is open,' he murmured. Then straightening his back, he turned and left the hall, closing the door behind him.

Tom felt a horrible thumping in his chest, as if a bird were trapped in his ribcage, flapping to break free. *Could this be a trick, designed to make him show himself? But why should it be? The servant could have given him away to Sir Percy at any moment . . . and yet he had said nothing.* Tom would have to take a chance. Gingerly, he pushed open the lid of the strong box, holding his breath as it creaked on its hinges. His cramped muscles screamed in pain as he clambered out but in spite of everything, he felt a shiver of hope. He didn't care why the servant had helped him. He knew where Bessie was and that was all that mattered.

Tom knew he had to keep calm. And, most of all, make sure he wasn't seen leaving the house. He glanced warily behind him, expecting to feel a hand on his shoulder as he tiptoed towards the open window. It was only a short drop to the winter garden below. In a fraction of a second he was over the sill and sinking to his knees in cold, sharp snow.

Tom ran at a crouch down the line of hawthorn leading to the river, stifling a cry as a partridge rose from the hedge in a whirr of wings. The promise of early morning had faded and the river breeze was laced with ice. Tom had no idea where the water stairs or the boathouse lay but he could hear the river close by, grey and full with the tide running in.

It was colder in the boathouse than it had been in the cellar under FitzNigel Hall, and the only daylight a small barred opening in the back wall. To begin with Bessie had struggled against her prison – first with the door and then with the bars at the window, tearing her skin so that now her hands were bleeding and her face was stained with tears. Sir Jocelyn had promised that if she kept quiet, a boat would come to take her home but she hadn't believed him. She had shouted and screamed until her throat felt raw but now she had sunk into brooding despair. Hours had passed in this gloomy silence with only a heel of crusty cheese to ease the pain of hunger. *I've been deserted*, she thought, tears of indignation welling in her eyes. *What a mess I've got myself in!* She closed her eyes, hearing her mother's voice in her head: '*You're a will o' the wisp, Bessie. Your head is full of dreams.*'

On reaching the river, Tom gazed furtively up and down along the bank. A chill breeze rustled the trees, promising rain. He glanced quickly over his shoulder towards the Hall, alarmed at the dark tracks his boots had made in the smooth surface of the snow. Everything looked quiet, but at any moment now, Sir Percy might visit the cellar and find him gone.

He picked his way cautiously down the weed-slicked steps towards the strip of mud that remained exposed even when the tide was high. To the west he saw an untidy mound of barrels, humped under a crust of snow and to the east, a long windowless building with a double oak door facing the water. Tom stole softly around the boathouse, ears alert for any sound of pursuit. *Please God, let Bessie be here*. There were no windows to the side. Softly, he crept around to the back.

In the darkness of the boathouse Bessie suddenly leapt to her feet. She felt sure there was someone outside. She ran to the opening in the back wall and listened, her heart thudding with hope. On the other side of the wall, Tom rose up on the tips of his toes and peered in. A pair of large frightened eyes peered out and stared directly into his.

Sir Percy FitzNigel smiled to himself as he waved his hand at Sir Jocelyn's departing figure. He had taken him on a tour of the new house. It really wouldn't do to fall out with Melchior now poor Caspar was dead. Sir Percy had the casket, after all. He smiled to himself. *Balthazar – The Lord of Treasure! How fitting a name for him! Oh but they'd shared some dangerous times together, he and Melchior. A pair of old rogues together!*

He took the broad stone steps in front of his new home two at a time, crossed the threshold and pushed open the door of the grand hall. *What uncommon luck*, he thought, remembering his earlier visitors. He could hardly believe it. The fools from Saint Agnes had played right into his hands! He heaved a great sigh and flung himself down at his desk, idly picking up the half finished letter to the Lord Chief Justice. It had been a sticky business with the casket. Perhaps they had been too greedy this time – gone for too rich a prize. But then again . . . He gazed around at his grand stone hall with its rich hangings of embroidered silk. It suddenly seemed small and mean. When he was Lord Chief Justice he would build another house. A palace to rival the Bishop of London's!

Sir Percy picked up his quill to complete the letter then narrowed his eyes with a frown. There was something black and sticky at the edge of the parchment. It looked like tar. He cast his eyes over the desk alighting on the strong box standing by the side. The lid was wide open. He jumped up from his chair and peered in. Some rolls of spare parchment in the bottom looked squashed, as if someone had been sitting on them. A chill breeze from the window lifted Sir Percy's hair. He spun round in irritation. Who had left a window open in this weather? In a moment he was peering into the snow drift, gazing in alarm at the large indentation and the tracks leading along the garden wall and down towards the river.

With a cry, Sir Percy bounded down the hall towards the blazing hearth, kicking away the straw that covered the trapdoor to the cellar. He could see black smudges around the edge of the square in the floor. He hauled on the iron ring. A damp riverish smell hit the back of his nose as he stared in dismay at the pyramid of barrels.

'Thomas Fletcher!' he snarled, stamping his foot. He'd

only this moment learned the boy's name, and now the wretch had escaped!

There was no way out for Bessie; that much was soon clear. The opening in the back wall was far too small. Tom rushed round to the doors of the boathouse and wrenched and pulled until his hands throbbed with pain, but the heavy oak doors were padlocked.

'Hurry Tom!' cried Bessie. 'I can't stand it in here much longer!'

'Don't panic! It's going to be all right!' called Tom through the door as he inserted his dagger into the lock and twisted hard. The tip snapped off with a crack. Tom groaned in frustration. He raced back to the window and clutched her hand through the bars. 'I'll get you out somehow – I promise! Don't despair, Bessie, there's good news. Your father's in London, I'll run and fetch him right away!'

Hastily Tom told her what he'd found out about the Three Wise Men. 'There are only two of them since Sir Percy killed Brother Gideon but they're up to all kinds of things – smuggling, forgery, even poisoning! My God, Bessie, they wanted to shut us up because we saw Sir Jocelyn murder those priests for the relic. Imagine if Sir Percy knew what I just overheard! But I'm in terrible danger now!' And then Tom outlined the news of the accusations against him back home.

'What can this relic be that men are prepared to kill for it?' whispered Bessie.

'I've an idea but there's no time to explain. All I know for sure is *I'm* accused of stealing it!'

For a moment their eyes locked. 'I'm scared for you, Tom,' said Bessie. 'You'll hang if you don't clear your name! You must hurry and fetch my father.'

Tom started suddenly. There was a cry from up at the house. Then the crackle of branches and running feet!

'He's staying at *The Mule* in Fish Street Hill,' hissed Tom as he backed away. 'I don't know where it is but I'll find it! I promise!'

Fear gave wings to Tom's feet. He ran like the wind, twigs cracking and his own hoarse breath loud in his ears. He flicked a glance behind but no pursuer had appeared on the riverbank. There was no time to lose. What if they moved Bessie again before he got back with her father?

The tide was high, slapping blackly against the river bank and as bad luck would have it, it had started to rain. He must remember what the backs of the houses looked like so he could lead Bessie's father to the right place. Before long he had reached The Strand, the long curving road that followed the line of the Thames between Westminster and London. Tom recognized the road. He'd been there before with Bart.

From Fleet Bridge Tom ran swiftly along City Wall, face aching and hands numb with cold, past the great bulk of Saint Paul's and down the hill towards Walbrooke. Swarms of people were milling around and Tom found the press of wet bodies a comfort. It was good to get lost in a crowd. He must be nearing London Bridge now. He might as well knock on Bart's door and ask him the way to *The Mule*. Tom quickened his pace, dashing the rain from his eyes as he ran. What might they do to Bessie if they looked in the cellar and found him gone?

As Tom sprinted towards London Bridge, leaping over dogs and dodging gingerbread sellers scurrying for shelter, he'd long ago stopped looking over his shoulder. He had no idea he was being followed . . . that other feet were running, softly, silently behind him.

Chapter 22

The Priest of Zarathustra

Abbot Swithin stood in the nave of the great Abbey of Westminster and gazed up at the leaking roof, held up by a forest of pillars. Vespers were over and the worshippers had gone. He was quite alone. He bent to adjust a wooden bucket. He might as well be in a real forest for all the rain the roof kept out.

The abbot heaved a weary sigh. He had three pressing problems. The first was what to do about the corpse of Brother Gideon, the sacrist, lying cold on a slab in the crypt. He couldn't keep the body forever, but an inquiry was plainly required and the sheriff was out of London, the Lord Chief Justice was ill and his second in command, Sir Percy FitzNigel, refused to take the matter seriously. Already there was a stench of decay however much incense he burned.

The second problem was connected with the first. Brother Gideon had acquired a mysterious relic that he had promised to present to the abbot on Christmas Day. How he had come by the relic, Brother Gideon had refused to say. And now it seemed the abbot would remain forever in the dark, since Christmas Day had passed, Brother Gideon was dead and the relic had disappeared without trace. And the third problem? Abbot Swithin was dying.

He had always been a good man, some even said saintly; a rare thing in the City of London. But now he was sick and old. His once straight back was bowed like a hoop and his whistling breath seemed to have sprung a leak in sympathy with the abbey roof. How had his life slipped by so fast? And now it was almost done – a painful thought which brought him back to the reason why he was feeling depressed. For Abbot Swithin was convinced that he had wasted his life; that he had not made his mark.

Some said he was a scholar and yet he had written nothing of value. Some said he was a saint and yet the Abbey of Westminster had not grown in glory under his leadership. Far from it, since the shrine of Saint Thomas at Canterbury was stealing his pilgrims in their thousands every year. There was no shortage of cripples and beggars of course but they didn't help mend holes in the roof. It was the rich they needed to win back – the ones who would pay for miracles with gold.

The solution was clear: the abbey needed a new relic to keep the flames of faith alive. But it had to be something better than the feather of the angel Gabriel's wing which everyone knew had once belonged to a white pigeon. And then all of a sudden – there had come a glimmer of hope.

It was almost a week ago, in the damp crypt of the abbey

that Brother Gideon had come with a proposal. Abbot Swithin had never liked Brother Gideon, so it was with some distaste that he saw the fat sacrist, padding like a toad towards him under the low vaulting arches, his heels together and his feet turned out. And yet the news he brought was far from disagreeable. A rare and precious relic had come into his hands. It was a treasure that would solve all the abbey's problems in the time it would take a leper to creep up and touch Edward the Confessor's tomb. And Brother Gideon was prepared for Abbot Swithin to have it – to take all the glory of acquiring it for himself. Abbot Swithin could make his mark at last. But as with everything to do with Brother Gideon . . . there was a price to pay.

'*It is well known that you are nearing the end of your life,*' Brother Gideon had said. '*But I have a proposition for you. I will give you this most precious relic in return for your solemn vow. That when the time comes for you to nominate your successor as abbot, your choice will be me! You have nothing to lose and everything to gain. You will be famous and your name will be blessed for evermore. And on your death, with the aid of this relic, I will become abbot of one of the richest abbeys in Christendom. Say nothing to anyone until you have come to a decision. But be sure of this. The relic now locked in the sacristy cupboard is worth a thousand times its weight in gold, so do not hesitate too long.*'

Abbot Swithin had demanded to see this relic. He had never trusted Brother Gideon, with his shifting eyes that never held a gaze, and besides, he knew him to be ambitious and greedy, unconcerned with the sick and the poor. But then again, think of the glory for the abbey! Honour was brought by the possession of relics. And so the sick old abbot reasoned round and round until his poor head was pounding – the promise of the relic always with him, glimmering at the edges of his vision.

But Abbot Swithin did not need to think for long. For it was the very next night that the watchman had come knocking at his door with the news of the body, a silken cord around its swollen neck, bumping softly against the river bank at the foot of Dead Man's Stairs.

Abbot Swithin gave a sudden start as a large splash of melted snow splattered on his black robe, shivering into tiny pearls and bringing him back to the present. How long had he been standing, alone in the nave, sunk in his gloomy thoughts? With a weary sniff, he hitched up his robe like a tavern wench and began to pick his way across the willow pallets placed over the larger puddles. The heady scent of incense had long faded and all he could smell was damp wood and plaster. But wait a moment. What was that curious scent? His thin nostrils quivered. And then suddenly he saw a figure, standing by the altar not two yards away – a dark-skinned man in robes of cinnamon-orange. And around his waist was wound a many-stranded silken cord, three knots along its length. As Abbot Swithin peered into the darkness, he recognized the smell. It was the sharp exotic scent of lemons.

Abbot Swithin's eyes were transfixed by the cord around the stranger's waist. He recognized it at once. To be sure, the cord he had pulled from around Brother Gideon's neck was slimy-green and slick with weed and this one was pure white as a new-born lamb but the three knots were just the same and at the end of the cord there hung a moonstone in the shape of a tear. The man in the cinnamon robe stared back, the smooth skin of his cheeks olive-gold in the candlelight, a small brand on his forehead in the shape of a flame. The frail old abbot shrank away, his hand to his throat, convinced that death had come for him.

Stepping softly forward, the stranger steepled his hands together under his finely arched nose and bowed low. Abbot Swithin's spirit flickered with an uncertain hope. The stranger's face was handsome, guarded but not unfriendly, with an expression of purity and intelligence which began to still the abbot's beating heart.

'Peace be upon you, Brother,' said the man in perfect English. 'I fear I have alarmed you. Do not be afraid, Abbot Swithin. I come in the hope that we might be of some use to each other. Pray allow me to introduce myself. My name is Shapur. I am a Zoroastrian astrologer priest from the ancient land of Persia, a follower of the prophet and sage, Zarathustra. Some call us magi, for we are renowned for our knowledge of magic and healing.' And so saying, he placed a gentle hand beneath the old abbot's elbow and led him to a low stone seat in the thickness of the wall.

'I come to you in hope that you might be able to help us retrieve a sacred treasure which is ours by right – a golden casket which was stolen by brigands from our Fire Temple high in the hills of my country. It is almost a year since our sacred temple was stormed, and in that time we have tracked our treasure through hills and valleys, by land and by sea, on foot and by camel caravan. A few weeks ago we followed it to a perfume bazaar in the ancient city of Cairo and there it fell into the hands of an unscrupulous relic hunter, a savage and ruthless knight, known in the east as *The Man with the Silver Finger*. From Cairo we followed him to your cold dark island and thence to London where he delivered our treasure into the hands of one of your monks, whom we would call *guardian of relics*.'

Abbot Swithin started visibly at the reference to Brother Gideon. 'We have no such relic here,' he said. 'You are mistaken. The casket which you seek is no longer with us and the sacrist you mention lies cold and dead in the crypt . . . strangled with a cord such as you wear around your robe!'

Now it was the priest's turn to tremble. 'What deed of darkness is this?' he said with a troubled frown. 'I had heard rumour of the monk's death but not until this moment the manner of it.' He shook his head in disbelief. 'Small wonder you shrank back in fear when you first saw me. But believe me, it is not as it must appear. This cord is the symbol of our religion, the Kusti, worn by all the followers of our prophet. Such a guardian cord was wound three times around our sacred casket. Each knot is a symbol of the three principles of Zarathustra's teaching – *good words, good thoughts, good deeds*.' He caressed each knot of the cord around his waist with his fingers. 'To think that a sacred cord of ours was used for such a purpose!'

Abbot Swithin nodded. He had read of the prophet Zarathustra. This casket the priest spoke of must surely be the relic that Brother Gideon had shown him. He gazed at the priest, his face alive with curiosity. 'Pray what is the significance of this casket for you?'

'I will tell you,' Shapur replied, seating himself down beside the abbot in the niche of stone. The dark priest smelt strongly of lemons. 'It is the holy ointment we all must wear,' smiled the priest, in response to the abbot's curious sniff. 'In homage to our prophet Zarathustra who received his knowledge sitting under a lemon tree. All followers wear the waxy balm. I must confess we find the stench of your city hard to bear.'

The abbot inhaled deeply, breathing in the heady scent. It was pleasant and there was something soothing too about the priest's melodious voice. 'Our religion is older than any on earth,' began the priest. 'We believe in the great god Ahuru Mazda, the creator, and in Ahriman, the spirit of all that is evil. Many hundreds of years before the birth of Jesus, the holy prophet Zarathustra was born to a virgin and all of Ahuru Mazda's creation rejoiced. One blessed day our prophet received the divine wisdom that is the foundation of our beliefs. He foretold that three *saoshyants* would come to earth, saviours from the regions of the dawn. The first would be announced by a wondrous star in the sky and the third and last would be the reincarnation of Zarathustra himself and he would found justice and truth on earth.'

Abbot Swithin nodded. 'I am a scholar and know something already of your religion. Pray tell me what this has to do with the casket.'

'Now when Jesus was born in Bethlehem in the days of King Herod,' the priest continued, 'three magi of

170

Persia's ancient faith followed a wondrous eastern star to the manger in Bethlehem. They were high priests of Zarathustra and they brought with them three gifts for the one whom we believe was the first promised saoshyant. The first gift was myrrh, a costly perfume and the Persian mark of a healer. The second was frankincense, which we Zoroastrians sprinkle on our sacred fire in honour of the one god, Ahuru Mazda.'

Abbot Swithin nodded. He knew the incense well. He had to burn it all day long to mask the smell of the corpse of Brother Gideon in the crypt!

'And the third gift was a golden casket,' continued Shapur. 'The tool of a magi's craft, and a traditional gift to a Persian king. Legends abound as to what happened to the three precious gifts the magi gave to the baby but the truth as we believe it is this; they were stolen by the disciple called Judas, and the Angel Gabriel appeared to the magi after Jesus' death and told them where the gifts were to be found. Find them they did, and these three gifts we now revere in our Fire Temple – or at least we did until the golden casket was stolen from us.'

In all this time, Abbot Swithin's eyes had not left Shapur's face. There was something compelling about this softly spoken priest. The abbot shifted his weight on the cold stone seat.

'You are cold,' said Shapur with concern.

'It is no matter,' replied the abbot with the briefest shake of his head. 'Pray continue your tale.'

'Since the theft of our sacred treasure I have travelled with two companions, also high priests of Zarathustra and together we came to London in pursuit of the casket. But once here, we suspected it had been removed from London by a visiting monk from a coastal abbey. Up until this time we had always travelled in threes, three being our sacred number; three knots, three gifts, three saviours. Yet someone had to remain behind in case our suspicion proved false whilst the others went in pursuit of our treasure. I was the one who remained. And now I have reason to believe that the casket is back in London – again in the possession of the silver-fingered knight. But of my companions, I have heard not a word. And now, alone and friendless in a foreign city, I begin to fear that they have met with some disaster.'

'I am sorry for you,' said Abbot Swithin in a low voice, 'but I do not see how I can help. What would you have me do?'

The priest placed his elegant hand on the abbot's age-flecked fingers. 'You are old and frail but as abbot of Westminster Abbey, you are still a man of influence. If you could help me find this ruthless knight and retrieve the casket which belongs to my people, I believe it could lead you to the murderer of your sacrist, Brother Gideon, and perhaps it might also help me to find my friends.'

Chapter 23

The Pastry Shop

'Ouch!' cried Tom, leaping over a pile of glowing cinders that had appeared out of nowhere and landed in his path.

'Sorry, mate!' shouted the man with the empty pan. 'It's the only way to melt the ice on my doorstep.'

Tom bent down and rubbed his shin where the hot sparks had burned through his britches, panting heavily with the effort of running so fast. He'd found London Bridge without trouble and since passing over the first arch, he'd been hugging the wall, keeping close in under the overhanging storeys of the houses. The noise of the water pounding through the narrow arches was deafening. He glanced behind him for the hundredth time, wondering about the shout he had heard back at FitzNigel Hall.

Crossing the busy thoroughfare, he gazed anxiously up at the wooden carving of a pie overhanging the pastry shop just above horse's head height. Next door but one was the rope maker's, a twisted rope like a hangman's noose above the lintel. The low door in the middle was Bart's.

It was little more than a hovel. The shutters were rotten, stuffed with rags to keep out the wind, and where the rags had run out there were gaping holes like eyes. Tom thumped urgently on the door, and then pressed his ear to the uneven planks. To his enormous relief he heard a scuffling sound from inside. A moment later a shutter creaked open and a small pinched face peered out. Tom darted to the window. It was a girl with a tangle of dirty black hair and an old-young face just like Bart's and the same thick eyebrows, although hers didn't meet in the middle.

'Is Bart at home?' blurted Tom. To his dismay the girl disappeared. 'Tell him it's Tom,' he shouted through the shutter. 'I'm . . . I'm a friend. I need to talk to him. It's urgent!'

Tom pressed his ear to the door again. 'Please open up!' he pleaded. But all he could hear was the scraping sound of something heavy being dragged across the floor. He raised his fist again, pausing at the scrape of a rusty bolt. There was the sound of someone jumping and then the door swung open in a cloud of smoke. Tom felt faint with relief.

'Sorry,' said the small girl. She was a female version of Bart, only half the size, and with a slight cast in one eye, so that whilst one looked at Tom, the other seemed to wander off in search of something else. 'I can't reach the bolt unless I climb up on the stool an' Bart says we've to lock ourselves in when he's not here.'

Tom's heart sank. *Not here*! He peered into the gloom.

The floor was thick with dirt and grease, smoke billowing from a small sputtering fire. 'Where is he?' asked Tom, gazing around. The air oozed damp and smelt sour and there were patches of mould on the walls.

'He's out. There's only me and little Meg at home,' said the girl, stooping over a small bundle that looked about three who was stirring a leather bucket with a pole. 'Ain't that finished yet, Meggie?' she said gently. The older girl thrust her hand in the bucket and pulled out a wooden crucifix dripping with red-coloured water. 'For the monks at the great Abbey at Westminster,' she said by way of explanation. 'Somebody there carves 'em , then we dye 'em and then they sell 'em to the pilgrims. It don't pay much but I can do it from home and look after Meggie at the same time.'

'Is your father around?' said Tom, trying to sound calmer than he felt. *Maybe* he'd *know the way to The Mule.*

The girl made a kind of choking face and put both her hands round her throat. 'Hanged!' she said, in a matter-of-fact voice.

Tom's hand flew instinctively to own his neck. 'Hanged!' he gasped. He swallowed hard, remembering Sir Percy's words. 'But I thought Bart said . . .'

'For stealing a loaf from the baker's in Bread Street,' explained the girl. At the look on Tom's face she sighed, folding her arms in an old-womanish way. 'So what's Bart been tellin' you then? I wouldn't take no notice of 'im if I was you. His tales are as long as this 'ere bridge! Our Ma used to scold 'im rotten for fibbing. But she's dead now too – so there ain't no one to remind him to tell the truth 'cept me.' The girl shrugged her thin shoulders. 'But we're all right, aren't we, Meggie?' she went on, with a proud tilt of her chin. 'We got our Bart to look after us, see. He's that clever. He gets enough money for all of us one way and another. Only never ask 'im how. He don't like it if we ask 'im how he gets 'is money!'

'Please tell me where I can find him.' interrupted Tom. 'I need his help. It's urgent.'

As if on cue, there was a knock on the door. 'Open up, Martha! It's only me!'

Martha's strange eyes lit up with pleasure. Little Meggie squirmed in her arms at the sound of her brother's voice. 'Bart! Bart!' she chanted, her thumb in her mouth.

'The door's open,' Martha called. 'You've got a visitor. He's in a hurry!'

The door clattered open and in stomped Bart, blowing on his hands and stamping his feet, Flea at his heels. At the sight of Tom, Flea let out a yelp of delight and before Tom knew it he had Flea in his arms, the grime of the last day disappearing under the lashing of his huge pink tongue. Bart stepped back in surprise. For a moment Tom saw a strange expression cross Bart's face; almost as if he wasn't too pleased to see him. But it was gone in a flash and Bart was slapping him on the back and grinning his broken-toothed grin.

'Now what 'appened to you last night in *The Three Cripples Inn*? You was there one minute and gone the next! You missed a good supper, didn't he Flea?' He crossed to the shutter and peered up and down the street. 'Not found your friend yet, then?' he asked in a casual voice.

'Well no. I . . . I mean yes . . .' stammered Tom, slightly unnerved by Bart's manner. He seemed strangely agitated and not nearly as friendly as before, but Tom pushed the thought to the back of his mind. He placed a struggling Flea on the floor. 'Listen Bart, can you direct me to *The Mule Inn*? I'm in a dreadful rush.'

Bart appeared to consider, scratching his head with a frown. 'Er . . . er . . . *The Mule*?'

'You know *The Mule*, Bart!' exclaimed Martha. 'At the top of Fish Street Hill. It's not far.'

Bart seemed confused for a moment and then suddenly his face cleared. 'Oh yes,' he said, slapping his forehead. 'I'd forgotten for a minute. You wait here while I get the girls some dinner from the pie shop next door and then I'll take you there meself.'

'There's really no need. Just tell me where it is . . .' began Tom, but before he'd finished his sentence, Bart was gone, slamming the door behind him.

Bart was away for some time. Tom stood by the door, tapping his foot impatiently whilst he talked to Martha, but at last the door crashed open again and Bart came in with an armful of piping hot pies. He was sweating although it was freezing outside.

'What took you so long?' exploded Tom. 'I told you I'm in a hurry. I need to find *The Mule*!'

'Sorry,' said Bart with a lopsided grin. 'Everyone wanted pies today!'

'Tom's been telling me his troubles,' said Martha. 'We've had a nice chat. Old friends, ain't we Tom?'

Tom said a hasty goodbye to Martha and scurried

outside after Bart. For some reason Bart seemed to have changed his mind about taking Tom to *The Mule*. Now he would only tell him the way. Tom hopped from one foot to the other as he listened impatiently to the instructions, then, mumbling his thanks, he sped off in the direction Bart pointed.

Repeating the route in his head, Tom elbowed his way through the press of bodies. Before long he was in a less crowded part of the city, hurrying through streets more miserable than any he had yet seen. The empty alleys made Tom nervous. He paused suddenly and glanced fearfully over his shoulder.

Something must be wrong.

Bart's sister had said it wasn't far to *The Mule* and yet he'd been walking for ages. Maybe he'd misunderstood the directions. There was something else odd too. Sir Ranulf de Lacy was rich, so why would they choose lodgings in such a dismal part of the city? This was a stinking place full of butcher's shops. He passed a great pool of blood, the surrounding snow spattered with crimson. Then all at once at the turn of a corner he saw two chequered stone towers with bars on the windows above an ugly gateway in the city wall. Beside the gate was a sinister wooden door with a spy flap.

Something was definitely wrong.

The tight ball of panic that had been steadily growing inside him rose up to his throat and the hairs stood up on the back of his neck. Tom stared wildly back down the deserted street from where he'd just emerged. Then all of a sudden he heard the sound of swiftly running feet and the clatter and clank of a chain. He whirled around but before he had time to take in what he saw, he felt a blow on the back of his head. His feet slipped from under him and he plummeted forward, falling to the ground and cracking his head on a stone.

Back in the hovel on London Bridge, Bart chewed on his pie, lost in thought.

'He seemed nice, Bart,' said Martha, wiping her mouth on her sleeve. 'He spoke so genteel.'

Bart looked up. 'Who seemed nice?'

Martha folded her arms and stared at him. 'What's got into you today? You're miles away! That poor boy what's going to be hanged if they catch him.'

Bart gave a violent start. 'Who's gonna be hanged?' he asked sharply, the colour draining from his face.

'That friend of yours what's just been here. Tom. He told me all about it and about his poor friend what's going to be shipped off to Africa for a slave.'

'What you talkin' about, Martha? Who's going to Africa?'

'Tom's friend, Bessie. I hope he finds her father before they ship her off to be sold. And if he can't find Bessie in time, then there's no one to clear his name and he'll be hanged at the horse pond! He told me about it while you took so long at the pie shop.'

Bart's face was now completely ashen, drained of all colour. Martha looked at him oddly, her head on one side. 'What's up Bart? You look as if you've seen the ghost of our dead mother!' She frowned. 'Come to think of it – what did take you so long at the pastry shop?'

Chapter 24

The Mule Inn

Tom came to with a start. He lifted his face from the filthy straw and stared round in bewilderment. The stench of the latrine mixed with that of unwashed flesh was overpowering. A stab of pain shot through his head, as if a blacksmith's hammer was striking inside his skull. His body felt heavy and he was very cold. He tried to touch his head, feeling at once the bite of cold iron on his wrists and hearing the rattle of the manacles. When he tried to sit up, he found his feet were shackled to a chain on the floor. He shuffled to a sitting position, peering into the grey shadows. Somebody moaned and a mound of rags by the wall heaved over, swore an oath – and then went back to sleep.

Where was he now? Tom forced his mind to focus. He'd been on his way somewhere. But where? His head pounded like a gallows drum. Slowly the veil began to lift. He'd been on his way to an inn; that was it. It was afternoon and he was trying to find Bessie's father.

'Oh, God,' he groaned aloud. 'Bessie!'

'Shut yer mouth over there!' came a beery voice.

A large man in a worn leather jerkin sat slumped on a stool, his elbows on a table in a small pool of light from a flickering oil lamp. There was a wooden tankard in front of him, its shadow huge on the stone wall behind, and above the shadow there was a small barred window high up near the ceiling. On the table next to the tankard was a vast iron ring, like a necklace of keys.

'Where am I?' shouted Tom, his stomach a knot of fear. 'There's been some mistake!' He tried to stand up but the fetters held him fast and he crumpled to the ground, face down in the matted straw.

The gaoler let out a great drunken laugh ending in a belch. 'That's what you all say when you first come to Newgate Prison, but you soon learn it don't do no good. You all swing in the end, if you don't starve to death first!'

Tom's eyes grew wide. How had he ended up here? He furrowed his brow as he tried to think of the last thing he remembered. *That was it!* He'd just been to see Bart and met his little sisters. Bart had told him the way to *The Mule* but somehow he'd lost his way. Suddenly Tom felt a rush of hot blood to his face as the truth dawned on him. How had he been such a fool when the evidence was there all the time? He'd just been too blind to see!

Who had been at Queen's Hythe when he left *Los Tres Magos* on Christmas Day? Who had taken him to see Sir Percy FitzNigel, and received four pennies for his trouble? Tom groaned in fury and thumped the floor with his fist. He'd thought the Justice's gesture was odd at the time, but he'd been too worried about Bessie to pay it any heed! Who had taken him to *The Three Cripples Inn* where he'd been captured? And who had directed him to *The Mule Inn* to meet Bessie's father and sent him into yet another trap?

Bart! Loneliness had made Tom blind. And now he remembered the expression of surprise on Bart's face when he'd turned up at his lodgings this afternoon. Tom should have smelt a rat then. What was it his sister had said? Bart's tales were as long as London Bridge!

'That little wretch and his dancing dog!' snarled Tom, tears of rage stinging his eyes. 'He's an informer for FitzNigel!' Tom groaned as he lay on the lice ridden straw. He'd been tricked. And now he would hang! He'd never see Bessie again.

Bessie was cold, so cold. But it didn't matter. Nothing mattered now. She was in a rowing boat on the Thames, her black hair flying and Tom was pulling on the oars. All around her were barges and little cogs with white and ochre sails. She could smell the salt tang of the estuary and the gulls overhead were diving and scavenging and the breeze whipped the waves into little crests of white foam. The wind lifted Tom's auburn hair and a strand blew over his freckled face. 'We're free, Bessie,' he laughed, his broken tooth glinting in the sun. 'I'm not going back to the abbey. We'll sail to Flanders and we'll never see London again!'

Bessie sat up and rubbed her eyes. It was dark, so dark it almost hurt. For a moment she was still in the dream, wondering why the sun had gone in and then she woke with a sickening jolt as she remembered her terror after Tom had left her. Sir Percy's men couldn't have been far behind him as he sped towards London. They'd arrived at the boathouse only minutes after Tom had gone, twisting her arms cruelly and shouting questions in her face. They were convinced Tom had been there – they'd followed his tracks from the house. But Bessie pretended she'd been sleeping. In spite of their brutal threats, she'd given nothing away. *Had Sir Percy's men caught up with Tom yet?* She felt sure that they must have done. He'd been gone for hours!

Bessie scrambled to her feet from the rotten rowing boat where she'd curled up in misery to sleep. She clambered on the prow to peer out of the tiny opening. It was afternoon when Tom had left her and now the moon was high. *Something terrible has happened to him*, she thought with a shiver of cold fear. *If they capture him again before he finds Father he will surely hang! And he can't have found him . . . or he'd have come for me by now . . .*

A tawny owl flew by with an eerie cry, its ghostly form silhouetted against the moonlit sky. Bessie trembled. *An omen of death.*

In Bart's house on London Bridge, Martha rocked little Meg in her arms. 'What's the matter, Bart?' she said, smoothing the little girl's hair. 'Is it about your friend what's in trouble?' The room was cold, the fire only glowing embers now, and it was dark too; just half a tallow candle, guttering in a puddle of wax.

'Nuffink,' said Bart sulkily. 'I've told you. It's nuffink.'

Martha pouted. She didn't believe him. 'Tell us a story then,' she urged. 'Tell Meggie the one about Saint George and the Dragon.'

'Dragon! Dragon!' cried Meggie, pulling her thumb from her mouth.

'No!' snapped Bart crossly, pressing the heels of his hands into his eyes. 'I'm tired. Can't you see? Leave me alone.'

Martha frowned. 'There *is* something wrong. You're not yerself. What is it? Are you worried about money? We've got enough for the rent, 'aven't we? You 'aven't lost that job 'ave you – the one wiv Sir Somebody-or-other?'

Bart slammed his fist hard on the table. 'No I ain't, and stop nagging, Martha! I'm goin' out wiv Flea. I need some air, that's all.'

'It's foggy out,' persisted Martha. She got up anxiously and closed the shutter. 'It's filthy out there.'

'Well I'm goin',' he snapped, getting up. 'I need to think. Put Meggie to sleep but don't go to bed yourself. When I come back there's somefink I might want you to do.'

It was dark in FitzNigel Hall, the only light came from the fire and the candles in the iron sconce by Sir Percy's desk. Fog from the river enveloped the water stairs and the boathouse and was now creeping up the garden outside his window. Sir Percy opened the shutter, surprised to see mist swirling thickly between the bare branches of the trees. It was too late to send a rider tonight, especially in this evil-smelling fog. He would write his letter now and send it first thing, in good time for the morning session.

The Justice straightened his woollen nightcap and gathered his fur lined cloak about his long elegant frame. He smiled to himself as he wrote, his goose feather quill travelling swiftly across the creamy parchment.

My dear Sir Ranulf,

Greetings! This letter brings both good tidings and bad. The good news is that I have laid hands on the rebel novice of whom you spoke. He is safe in Newgate Prison and will be tried today in Westminster Hall at ten. Your presence and that of the girl's father are required to bear witness against him. Since the Lord Chief Justice is unable to leave his bed, I myself will preside.

I regret that there is as yet no news of your granddaughter, but you may rest assured that if any tidings of her reach my ears, I will be the first to inform you.

Sir Percy licked his teeth in satisfaction. "'I remain,' he muttered, dipping his quill into the pot of brown ink on his desk, 'your humble servant, Sir Percy FitzNigel, Justice to His Majesty, the King".'

Sir Percy shook sand over the parchment. That would do the trick! He'd thought the game was up when he'd found the empty cellar but thankfully all was well. That urchin with his scruffy mongrel had been more useful than he'd ever thought possible. Money very well spent! By this hour tomorrow that meddling novice would be dead – and the girl would be on her way to Africa.

The Mule Inn was so lopsided it looked as if it were about to give up the struggle to stand upright and come crashing down into the street. However there was a hearty fire inside, a cauldron of hot cider and a dish of gulls' eggs for the anxious travellers. Gabriel Miller sat hunched in his cloak, his trencher untouched on the table, brooding eyes fixed on the flames as they hissed and crackled in the hearth.

'Come, Master Miller,' urged Fustian. 'You must take some food. You will not help your daughter by starving yourself.'

Gabriel Miller, looked up, his eyes red-rimmed with exhaustion. He had tramped the streets of London asking after Bessie at every drinking hole and tavern. He had even tried the hospital of Saint Bartholomew beyond the city wall. But all in vain.

'Where in God's name can she be?' he said in broken tones. 'I cannot return to Saint Agnes and face Alice without our daughter. I had no idea London was so vast.' He shook his head. 'The task is beyond us, Sir Ranulf. And yet there is something within me – some intuition that tells me she is not far away.' He brushed a tear from his cheek with the back of his hand. 'But perhaps that is only the foolish fancy of a despairing old man.'

The curfew bell sounded, and the landlord began to scuttle about the low beamed room, dousing the candles and preparing to bed down for the cold winter night, ushering the last reluctant stragglers through the door and out into the snow.

'We must away to our beds,' said Sir Ranulf with a sigh. 'There is nothing more to be done tonight. The sheets might be damp but they seem cleaner than many a tavern I have stayed in.'

There was a scuffle at the door and the sound of the

landlord's voice, suddenly raised in protest. A young girl was trying to squeeze through the departing forms into the room, close muffled against the freezing fog. Her head was bare and small flakes of snow clung like star-shine to her tangled dark hair. Once inside, she shrank back apprehensively, staring at the faces turned towards her in the firelight. She had a strange cast in her eyes.

'I've . . . I've brought a message,' she burst out, 'about a girl called Bessie Miller.'

Chapter 25

In the Monks' Graveyard

Gabriel Miller sprang to his feet. The girl cringed away and took a step backwards. 'If you . . . if you want to see her,' she gabbled, already at the door, 'you've to go to the monk's graveyard, hard by the Abbey at Westminster – tonight when the bell tolls one.'

Gabriel took a step towards the girl but she was too quick for him. Whirling on her heel, she darted through the door and was gone.

'Wait! Come back! Who sent you?' he cried, racing outside. With a groan of despair he gazed frantically up and down the alley. There were only a few cloaked figures to be seen, hurrying home to cover their fires. The girl was a spirit or she must have run like the wind. A choking winter fog had descended, thick and yellow-grey. Gabriel blinked into the swirling darkness but she was nowhere to be seen.

Gabriel and his companions wasted no time. Within

minutes they had donned their cloaks and riding boots and were racing to the stables to saddle their mounts. And before long, three muffled horsemen were trotting quickly through the deserted waterfront fish market of Thames Street. Sir Ranulf led the way, holding a storm lantern aloft in one hand, its sulphurous yellow light a fuzzy glow through the mist that hung thick and chill over the river. Gabriel Miller had prayed for news of Bessie, but now his spirit quailed with dread. *Who was the messenger girl and why had she disappeared without trace?* Something terrible had happened to Bessie; he felt it in the frozen marrow of his bones.

It was midnight. As the heavy bell of Saint Paul's tolled the end of the day, Gabriel prayed Sir Ranulf's purse was deep enough to bribe the gatekeeper at Ludgate. The curfew bell had clanged out long ago and now the only sounds were the horses' hooves on the hard-packed snow and the hiss of the river, sliding by on their left-hand side. However the chink of silver satisfied the gatekeeper, and soon they were riding under the arch of Ludgate towards the Fleet River below the city's western wall. Dimly, through the mist, they could just make out the red glare of fires that burned on the small craft moored beside the wharfs. Before long they were striking south, following the river's great bowing curve towards the city of Westminster.

Bartholomew Bucket had always had nimble fingers and his father had taught him all he knew before the slip-up in the bakery had cost him his neck. So not only was Bart one of the best cutpurses in London, he could pick any lock from The Tower of London to the Palace of Westminster. A mere boathouse would be child's play.

So as Sir Ranulf de Lacy led his party along The Strand to Westminster, Bart stood on the riverbank, peering back at FitzNigel Hall to make sure he was unobserved. Keeping to the shadow of the hedge, he crept down the water stairs to the beach, Flea clutched tight in his arms. Peering east along the foreshore, he could just make out the shape of the boathouse. 'Hush, Flea,' he said, setting the small dog down at his feet. 'Your job's to keep a look out!' He unlooped a leather sack from around his neck and emptied the contents onto the hard damp mud: one tinderbox, the brown stub of a candle, one jar of oil, a curved metal wiggler, one straight jiggler and a wrench – the tools of his father's trade. Striking a flint with an expert hand, he breathed a spark into a flame, then selecting the straight jiggler, he dipped it in the oil and with a steady hand inserted it carefully into the lock.

Inside the boathouse Bessie sprang to her feet. 'Who's there?' she cried out. 'Tom! Is that you?'

'Keep quiet for God's sake!' hissed an unknown voice. 'It's a friend.'

The monks' graveyard was an eerie place, the yellow fog seething around the headstones like dead men's breath. Some of the tombs were broken and crumbling, some leaning at drunken angles over grassy mounds. The three companions tied their horses to a row of spiked railings by the lych gate, deep in the northern shadow of the abbey. Fustian stayed to mind the horses whilst Sir Ranulf and

Gabriel picked their way through pools of darkness towards the stone cross in the middle. They paused, stared round and listened. All was silent, except for the sound of their ragged breathing and the harsh cries of night birds.

Wordlessly they stood together, shoulder to shoulder in the near-dark, breathing in the smell of damp moss and earth mould. Watching. Silently waiting as the bell tolled one. Sir Ranulf's hand strayed to his sword. Gabriel's lips moved in silent prayer, his breath like a cloud of incense. *Please God, bring Bessie back.* What did he care for fine marriages? Bessie could marry a penniless farm hand for all he cared. Only let her be safe!

Bart glanced fearfully over his shoulder back towards the house. The lock was harder to pick than he'd expected and his best jiggler had snapped clean in two. *Why am I risking my neck for a girl I don't even know? God help me if FitzNigel sees me! Martha had better have taken the message.* Bart's pangs of conscience were fading rapidly, the longer it took him to pick the lock. He heard Martha's voice in his head: '*You can't let them ship her to Africa, Bart. What harm's she ever done you?*'

'Damn Martha!' he muttered under his breath. With trembling hands he selected the long wiggler, the one with the hooked end, and tried again. If it didn't work this time, he'd give up and go home.

Bart held his breath as he twisted the wiggler, his ear to the door, exhaling sharply as something clicked inside the lock. A split-second later, Bart was heaving on the boathouse door, kicking the banked-up snow away with his boots. On the other side of the door, Bessie backed away, her throat tight with fear. *Who was this stranger? Why hadn't Tom come himself and brought her father with him?*

The fog swirled in as the door shivered open in a flurry of snow. 'Who are you?' gasped Bessie. 'Did Tom send you? Is he all right?'

'Don't ask no questions – you'll get told no lies,' said the boy fiercely, dragging her out by the arm. 'I'm risking my life as it is! Make for the monks' graveyard up by the abbey. Your father should be waiting there.' He pointed along the beach. 'Cut along the bank and up the next water stairs. You'll see the abbey over the rooftops. Now scarper!'

Bessie stood rooted to the spot. There was so much she wanted to ask. Who was he? Who'd sent him? Was he anything to do with Tom? But before she had time to gather her thoughts, the boy had sprung away from her and was already racing along the beach in the opposite direction, disappearing into the thickening mist, a small shaggy dog scampering behind.

Bessie didn't run at once. She stood by the open boathouse door, gazing after the boy like a wild animal released from a trap, unable to believe in its freedom. *Her father! Close by! And was Tom with him too? But it didn't make sense. If her father was close by, why hadn't he come for her himself?* She looked uneasily over her shoulder – expecting to see Sir Jocelyn emerging through the mist – but there was no sound except the wind in the bare branches of the trees and the rush and gurgle of the Thames. *The monks' graveyard*, thought Bessie with a shudder. *Oh God, please let my father be there!*

It was so misty she could hardly see the river, let alone the water stairs the boy had mentioned. Clutching her cloak around her, she groped blindly along the bank, praying she wouldn't lose her footing in the dark. Before long, Bessie saw a dense shape, black against the river bank. She ran the last few steps, almost sobbing with relief as the wooden stairs took shape through the mist. They were little better than a ladder. She clutched her skirt in one hand and hauled herself up the steep rungs. At the top, she paused, listening to the thumping of her own heart. The boy said she would see the abbey but all she could see through the fog was an unlit alley leading away from a huddle of hovels that clung to the river bank.

Trying hard not to panic, Bessie crept past the huts with their threads of grey smoke and smells of boiled cabbage. The curfew bell had long since tolled its warning and the dingy lane was deserted, although she could see candle light through chinks in the ramshackle shutters of some of the miserable dwellings. Should she bang on a door and ask the way? She half raised her fist to knock at the first door. From inside came the thin hungry wail of a baby and a gruff voice, raised in anger. She dropped her hand to her side and then leapt back with a shriek as something black brushed past her leg and streaked away into the night. It was only a cat but Bessie was trembling, her pent-up nerves stretched like a gallows rope.

Furtively, she crept down the misty alley, her eyes darting from window to window until she emerged onto a broader street of hard-packed ice. She hadn't noticed the shadowy form that had uncoiled itself from a doorway as she passed. Suddenly a hand grabbed her shoulder!

Bessie screamed.

'Well, well, what a surprise!' came a voice, thick with ale. 'Now what's a pretty wench like you doin' out on a filthy night like this? You should be tucked up in bed.' Bessie struggled in the man's iron grasp. His fingers were digging into her neck and she could smell his stale breath and the stench of the unwashed. She cried out in disgust as he pressed his mouth close to her ear. 'How about comin' to *One-Eyed Jack's* along with me now?' he said in a throaty whisper. 'I'll soon warm you up!'

For a moment Bessie stood paralysed, like a hare caught in a trap, and then with a cry, she sank her teeth into the man's hand. He let go, yelping in pain and then she was off, bolting as fast as her legs could pump, away down the tangle of narrow alleys that led from the river. She fled like the wind, flicking a backward glance at the sound of pounding feet. The drunkard was gaining on her! At a bend in an alley, she paused to catch her breath and all at once she realised her mistake.

Her mind froze. She couldn't breathe. She couldn't think.

Her pursuer had stopped running now and was walking slowly towards her, grinning a broken-toothed grin, gaining on her step by step, as she backed away from him towards the blind end of the alley.

'Let me go! Let me go! Take your hands off me!' shrieked Bessie as the man steered her towards a tavern. 'Let me go!'

Bessie stared wildly around, praying someone would hear her cries – a night-watchman perhaps. The door of *One-Eyed Jack's* flew open in a roar of laughter, amber light flooding the frozen snow like liquid gold, and a drunken man lurched out followed by a woman with a painted face. Bessie's throat tightened. *What kind of a place* was *this*?

Bessie's captor pushed her into the smoky ale room, kicking the door closed behind him with his boot. Men were slouched on piles of sacks heaped together against the walls, swigging beer from hard leather tankards. Bessie gaped open-mouthed at the faces of the women. They looked so young – all cochineal lips and rosy cheeks – but as her eyes grew accustomed to the gloom, Bessie saw that their cheeks were sunken, and dark hollows ringed their eyes.

'Look what I found wanderin' outside all by herself!' leered the broken-toothed man, pushing Bessie into the yellow fug of smoking rushlights. The women glared at Bessie with hostile eyes. 'Well don't just sit there staring!' shouted the man. 'Fetch the little lady some ale!'

'I . . . I don't need ale,' Bessie stammered. 'I . . . I'm looking for the monks' graveyard. It's somewhere near the abbey, I think. Can anybody tell me the way?'

There was a titter of mocking laughter. 'The monks' graveyard!' jeered the man. 'Now what would a pretty wench like you want with a dead monk at this time of night?'

In the rat-infested straw of Newgate Prison, Tom stared despairingly at the foggy sky through the small barred window, high up above the slumbering gaoler's head. The keys to the gaol lay tantalisingly out of his reach on the table. He was so thirsty. His throat felt as if he had swallowed broken glass. He wanted to shout and scream; rage against the injustice of it all but he knew it would do no good. He had the information to clear his name. Information that could send de Maltby and FitzNigel to the gallows. And yet who would believe him at his trial without Bessie to speak up for him? Tom closed his eyes and tried to quell the fear that was constricting his throat like an iron fist. *Is Bessie still a prisoner in the boathouse or has de Maltby taken her already? By this time tomorrow she'll be on her way to Africa. And as for me?* The gaoler had told him he would hang in the morning. *By this time tomorrow, I'll be dead!*

Chapter 26

A Dishonourable Man

Sir Ranulf and his party had waited until the great bell of Westminster Abbey tolled three before reluctantly concluding that the squint-eyed girl had led them on a fool's errand. Gabriel had been reluctant to leave his post at the stone cross but Sir Ranulf had insisted that they had best return to their lodgings in case news of Bessie arrived whilst they were away. So within an hour, the three riders were trotting dismally back up Fish Street Hill to rouse the landlord of *The Mule* from his bed. He stumbled grumpily to the door in his weaselskin nightcap. If the nightwatch found him opening his door after curfew they'd close his establishment down! However, his temper was quickly restored by Sir Ranulf's silver and now the three companions crouched gloomily around a roaring fire, their backs cold but their faces warm.

'Something dreadful has befallen Bessie,' muttered the miller in a broken voice. 'Or else why did she not come?'

Sir Ranulf de Lacy gazed sadly at Gabriel, searching for some words of comfort. The miller looked smaller somehow, sunk into himself with grief. 'Have courage, Master Miller,' he said kindly. 'We must make enquiries about the messenger girl in the morning. Someone must know a girl with a squint-eye. And don't forget that the King's Justice promised faithfully to issue a description of Bessie. Perhaps the morning will bring some word from FitzNigel.'

At the mention of the Justice, Fustian let out a scornful snort. Sir Ranulf looked sharply at his clerk. 'It seems the very mention of Sir Percy sets your teeth on edge,' said Sir Ranulf. 'I know that you were glad to leave his service but I sense there is something else. What did you mean earlier on . . . when you said you did not think him a gentleman? Out with it, man!'

Fustian pursed his lips in irritation. After all, he had tried to warn his master earlier in the day, but Sir Ranulf had not let him speak.

'It is not for me to criticise my betters,' he mumbled. 'But the Justice is a dishonourable man.' He glanced uncomfortably at Gabriel Miller who was staring unblinking into the fire. Fustian lowered his voice. 'I mean I would not rely on him to help us.'

'Dishonourable?' said Sir Ranulf with a frown. 'That is a serious allegation against a King's Justice. Pray tell me what you mean.'

'He's up to all kinds of mischief that a man in his position ought not to be,' replied Fustian, pulling his moustache. 'He and his friends. Smuggling chiefly: bear skins and beaver pelts, Baltic amber – that sort of thing. They call themselves the Three Wise Men. Fellow students from their days at the University of Paris.'

Sir Ranulf looked surprised. 'I am shocked that a Justice to the King would run the risk of evading customs duties. I have never had much time for FitzNigel, but I thought him merely vain and stupid. And are these friends of his lawyers too?'

Fustian gave contemptuous laugh. 'One of the three is a powerful monk at the great Abbey of Westminster – the sacrist no less, by the name of Brother Gideon. As greedy a monk as ever took the vow of poverty!'

Sir Ranulf raised an eyebrow. 'And the third?'

'A knight named Sir Jocelyn de Maltby – a relic hunter known as *the Man with the Silver Finger*. They have a trading ship – *Los Tres Magos*. They think it the hugest joke. Three failed students with forged degrees from the University of Paris and a ship called *the Three Wise Men*! It takes only a little brine, dirt and oil for an expert forgery of a degree from Paris that it takes nine years to obtain by studying! Nowadays Sir Percy uses his skills to forge royal pardons for his friends and grants of land to himself.'

'Forged grants of land and royal pardons!' exclaimed Sir Ranulf. 'You amaze me, Fustian. He would hang if word of this got out!'

Fustian nodded. 'So now you understand why I say he is not to be trusted. He has made a small fortune for himself,' said Fustian bitterly. 'And he certainly doesn't share it around!'

* * *

At first Bessie had pleaded with the man with the broken teeth to let her go but instead he'd thrust a tankard of warm ale into her hand and dragged her down onto his knee, placing his arm around her waist in a vice-like grip. Bessie shrank into herself in revulsion, eyes fixed on the floor, hardly able to bear the hungry leers of the other men and the hostile whispers of the painted women. *If only I'd been more careful*, she thought bitterly. *If I'd looked behind me I might be with Father now.*

The air in *One-Eyed Jack's* was thick with wood smoke and tallow and Bessie's throat felt parched. Gingerly, she took a mouthful of ale. It was a surprisingly strong brew, especially after not having eaten for hours. And it was just as the powerful liquid was trickling down her throat and warming her empty stomach that Bessie had her idea. Her captor had been drinking heavily already – that much was obvious. Could she use her feminine charms to persuade him to drink a little more?

Bessie was wary of a woman with pocks on her face who seemed to think she was after her man, but really Bessie could think of nothing else to do. So summoning all her courage and fighting down waves of disgust, she tried to take long slow breaths, forcing her body to relax. With a shiver of distaste, she made herself snuggle up to her captor and leaning her head against his chest, tried to ignore the stink of his sweat. Gritting her teeth she smiled up at him from under her long eyelashes. 'Your tankard looks empty,' she said in a teasing voice. 'Why don't you let me fill it up?'

Bessie was careful not to drink any ale herself in spite of

her thirst as she sat on her captor's knee, attempting to nod and smile along with the bawdy jokes of the other men. From time to time she would prise the man's arm from her waist and get up to refill his tankard from the barrel, ignoring the spiteful glances of the pock-marked woman, until at last his head began to nod on her shoulder. The ale and the fuggy warmth of the fire had dulled his senses, and before long, his arm slid heavily from Bessie's waist. A few minutes more and she could hear his drunken snores.

Was the man fast asleep? Or would he wake as soon as she tried to escape? Hardly daring to breathe, Bessie had just begun to wriggle cautiously from under his arm, when suddenly the pock-marked woman stood up.

Bessie was not the only one who had been biding her time. The woman had been waiting for her opportunity too – to be rid of her pretty rival! And as soon as the man's snores settled into a regular rhythm she seized her chance. Poking the sleeping form with the tip of her boot, just to make sure he was dead to the world, she grabbed Bessie roughly by the arm and hauling her to her feet, she pushed her out through a filthy curtain at the back of the tavern and into the icy yard.

'Get out of here, you hussy,' she snarled. 'And don't yer never show yer face on my patch again!' She shoved Bessie hard in the back, sending her sprawling into the frozen midden heap at the back of *One-Eyed Jack's*. Bessie heard the tavern door bang shut behind her. She struggled to her feet, dusting snow from her cloak.

'Don't worry. I won't be back!' muttered Bessie under her breath.

With a sinking heart, she stared up at the leaden sky at the back of the tavern. The tower of Westminster Abbey loomed through the mist, dark grey against the paler tones of the winter sky. It was wonderful to be free again but her spirits failed as she thought of her father. It had been hours since the mysterious boy had freed her from the boathouse. Surely her father wouldn't have waited this long!

With the tower in view it was easy to find her way. The fog had lifted a little and as she hurried towards the abbey she heard the bell toll four. She paused, her hand on the cold lych-gate, and peered anxiously around the graveyard. Tears of frustration stung her eyes. She could just make out the snowy mounds of graves and the shapes of broken tombstones. There was not a living soul in sight.

Chapter 27

Gallows Fodder

Abbot Swithin had woken with a sneeze. He feared he was getting a cold. After breakfast he would ask his physician to rub his chest with oil of sage and parsley, but first he must open the abbey for prime, the service at first light. He had a busy morning ahead. Sir Henry de Mandeville, the Lord Chief Justice, had at last agreed to see him, to discuss serious matters regarding the murder of his sacrist, Brother Gideon.

The abbot's raw red nose preceded him like a fiery poker across the monks' graveyard as he hobbled painfully towards the arched porch of Westminster Abbey, his breath like puffs of smoke in the grey dawn air. He pulled his rabbit-lined cloak more closely about him, fumbling in its folds for the large iron key. Entering the abbey porch, he gave a start. There was a body, slumped on the stone bench that ran at waist height on two sides of the arched entrance. He shuffled nearer, leaning down to look into the sleeper's face. He stepped back in surprise. It was not the expected leper with his distinctive hood and bell, but a girl, and a pretty one at that.

Bessie awoke with a cry. She'd been dreaming of the man with the broken teeth. She shrank back, and then breathed a sigh of relief when she saw the figure was only a bent old monk, leaning down and peering into her face. She sprang to her feet. She had only intended to rest for a moment. She hadn't meant to fall asleep.

'Can you direct me to the *Mule Inn* in Fish Street Hill?' she asked anxiously. 'I need to go there right away.'

Abbot Swithin knitted his brow. *Why was a young girl like this sleeping rough in the abbey porch?* 'There is no Fish Street Hill in the town of Westminster,' he said with gentle concern. 'You'd best try the City of London, my dear. But that's two miles away. Pray let me take you to the abbey guest house. Our guest-master will be glad to give you food and shelter.'

Two miles! What was Bessie to do? She was worn out and her stomach was hollow with hunger. But there really was no choice. Her only hope of finding her father was to find *The Mule Inn* where Tom had said Gabriel was lodging. Bessie shook her head. She was grateful for his kind concern but she really couldn't wait.

'Then at least you must take my cloak,' urged Abbot Swithin. 'Your own will provide no warmth at all. I believe it is soaked through.'

Tears sprang to Bessie's eyes at the kindness of the frail old monk. *There's goodness in the world after all*, she thought as she gathered the abbot's warm cloak about her and summoned the last of her strength to trudge the two miles in the direction he had pointed, following the curve of the black river towards the City of London.

It was morning at last and the tradesmen of London were busy taking down their shutters and laying them horizontally across the front of their small shops to form a makeshift counter to sell their wares. They were too busy to pay any heed to the footsore girl with black hair who was dragging herself up Fish Street Hill, her limbs heavy with exhaustion. They were well used to the sight of beggars and this limping girl looked no different from the rest, although they might have looked twice had they known that her rabbit-lined cloak once belonged to the Abbot of Westminster Abbey.

In the parlour of *The Mule*, at the top of Fish Street Hill, Sir Ranulf de Lacy started awake from his doze in front of the embers of the fire. He and his companions had not troubled to go to bed. They had talked through the night as the fire had dwindled and the light of dawn began to streak the sky with paler grey. He stood up with a stretch and rubbed his eyes. Perhaps it was the noise from the street outside that had awoken him. He moved stiffly to the window, pressed the shutters aside and peered into the fine drizzle that had replaced the fog of the previous night. He narrowed his eyes. There was somebody out there; a hooded form in a dark woollen cloak. In a moment, Sir Ranulf was at the door, flinging it wide just as Bessie staggered against the lopsided door frame, swayed sideways and fell in a faint to the ground.

Before many minutes had passed, Bessie was huddled in dry blankets in front of a newly kindled fire, a bowl of mutton stew untouched on the bench by her side. She'd been faint with hunger when she'd arrived but now her stomach heaved at the very smell of food. She'd hoped for news of Tom and now she was sick with worry.

'I know you're angry with Tom, Father,' blurted Bessie. 'But it wasn't his fault. Believe me! Running away to London was my idea. He didn't want to take his vows but the idea of London was mine. Then we found ourselves caught up in all this! And now he stands accused of terrible crimes that are nothing to do with him. There's so much to tell I don't know where to begin.'

Gabriel Miller stared reproachfully at his daughter. 'Perhaps at the beginning, Bessie,' he said. 'I often find that's best.'

So Bessie told them all that had happened, from the time when she and Tom had witnessed the theft of the casket from Saint Wilfred's that fateful evening. She told how they'd accidentally set sail on *Los Tres Magos*, about the murder of the priests by the man with the silver finger and how he'd discovered her hiding on the boat. With tears of indignation, she told what she knew about Sir Percy FitzNigel and the murder of Brother Gideon, just as Tom had told it to her and of how he had escaped from FitzNigel Hall. She could only guess at what had befallen Tom on the way to find her father. He'd simply disappeared. 'All I know is that we're caught up in a dangerous web of murder and greed . . . and Tom's vanished! Something dreadful must have happened, or he'd have found you here. Oh Father, we have to do something!'

Gabriel Miller turned helplessly to Sir Ranulf de Lacy who slapped his hand on his knee. 'I do not know where to begin looking for your friend,' he said passionately, 'but there is certainly *something* we can do, knowing what we know now. Indeed we have a duty to tell what we have learned. One of these men is a knight of the realm and the other a Justice to His Majesty the King!' He scratched his grizzled beard. 'We must visit Sir Henry de Mandeville right away. Sick bed or no there are things about Sir Percy FitzNigel that a Lord Chief Justice has to know!' he paused and turned to the window, peering out into the street once again. 'That's curious,' he said. 'A rider is approaching and it looks as if he is coming here.' Sir Ranulf stepped out into the street, squinting through the drizzle.

'A message for Sir Ranulf de Lacy,' panted the rider leaning down. Sir Ranulf took the sealed parchment from his hand, pressing a coin into the rider's damp glove. He strode hurriedly back into the parlour, snapping open the seal.

Bessie sprang to her feet. 'Is it news of Tom?'

They all crowded round Sir Ranulf, lips moving silently as four pairs of eyes scanned the parchment.

'*My dear Sir Ranulf,*' they read, '*Greetings! This letter brings both good tiding and bad . . .*

Newgate Prison . . . will be tried today in Westminster Hall at ten . . . Sir Percy FitzNigel, Justice to His Majesty the King.'

'Newgate Prison!' whispered Bessie.

'Ten o'clock,' gasped Fustian as the church bells began

to clang. They all held their breath as the bells tolled the hours. Six . . . seven . . . eight.

'Eight o'clock,' breathed Bessie, her face white. 'Only two more hours until ten!'

Due east of Westminster Abbey, Tom Fletcher blinked in the driving rain, unused to the light after so many hours in his prison cell. The gaoler pushed him hard in the back and he stumbled the last few feet to the jetty, like an old man whose every step brings a stab of pain. His feet, newly free of the iron fetters, seemed to belong to someone else and his hands were still manacled in front of him. They were marching him down towards the river. He could hear its rushing tide and the cry of the gulls. It was a dark stormy morning of low drifting cloud.

From the river bank, Tom gazed forlornly at the painted boats with coloured sails bobbing on the water. It seemed odd to watch the world going on as usual whilst he lived through this nightmare. He felt utterly defeated. Almost losing his footing on the slippery water stairs, he had no choice but to allow himself to be bundled into a rowing boat. A man sat in the prow wearing an oilskin cloak and hat, oars at the ready as if he'd been waiting for some time. He grasped Tom by his chain without a word and manacled him to the stern.

'Westminster Stairs as quick as you can,' growled the gaoler, jangling his keys. 'There'll be somebody there to meet you. No need to wait to bring him back, though,' he said, jerking a fat thumb towards Tom. 'This one's gallows fodder!'

Chapter 28

In the Name of the King!

The central court of Justice, Westminster Hall, was a giant stone building near the great stone abbey and hard by the courtyards of the Royal Palace. A curious crowd had gathered outside the great ribbed door. It was most unusual for the court to be in session at Christmastide. Candles had been lit inside against the gloom although it was only midday, and yellow points of light shone through the high glass windows. The grey rain fell on the grey stone hall as people elbowed their way under the arched door into the cavernous space inside, scuffing up the rushes in their effort to get inside out of the rain.

There was, as yet, no sign of the King's Justice. A lawyer's clerk was already in his place, warming his hands at a candle. He sat on a stool at a table below the dais, rolls of parchment in front of him next to a pot of newly sharpened quills. He looked up sharply at the sound of jangling spurs. Sir Jocelyn de Maltby was striding between the two long rows of pillars that supported the immense roof. Eyes sliding right and left like the wily fox he was, the knight proceeded down the hall, his short beard sharp as a scimitar, and took his seat on one of the public benches.

The early morning drizzle had turned to driving rain by the time Sir Ranulf de Lacy rode into the courtyard of Sir Henry de Mandeville's grand stone house near Westminster Abbey. Golden candlelight shone from one of the upper windows. *I fear Sir Henry must still be abed*, he thought *I am sorry to intrude on him so early but I cannot delay any longer.*

In the upper chamber the Lord Chief Justice's face was thin and pale; his eyes hollow under his thick grey brows. They followed the physician's hands as he raised the jar of honey to his fleshy nostrils and sniffed, his eyebrows meeting in the middle in a deep frown of suspicion. 'There is no doubt in my mind!' said the doctor, exhaling with a shudder. 'The smell is unmistakeable. It is undoubtedly wormwood!'

Sir Henry's face paled further still and his hands clawed the bedclothes. 'But . . . but the honey was a gift . . .'

The plump physician raised his eyebrows. 'To begin with I felt sure your bodily humours were unbalanced,' he said gravely. 'Too much phlegm and black bile and not enough blood. Yet now I am convinced you are suffering from a disease of the stomach brought on by slow poisoning with toxic honey . . .'

He broke off. There was a sudden commotion outside

the door, the sound of scurrying feet and the voice of a manservant raised in protest. The Lord Chief Justice passed a weary hand over his scholarly face. 'Pray tell whoever it is that I can see nobody else this morning,' he sighed. 'The visit from Abbot Swithin of Westminster has quite exhausted me. All that news about relics and knights with silver fingers! I have had quite enough for one morning.' He groaned in pain, clutching his stomach. 'I am harried to within an inch of my life – legal cases backing up when I am not in health to deal with them.'

There was an urgent knock. The physician moved quietly to the door, prepared to send the visitor away, but before he could open his mouth, Sir Ranulf de Lacy whirled past him into the room almost bowling him to the ground. 'Pray forgive the intrusion at so early an hour, Sir Henry,' blurted Sir Ranulf de Lacy, 'but I fear this is an affair that cannot wait. It is a matter of life and death!'

Tom Fletcher stood in the corridor behind the door that led to the Court of the King's Bench, flanked by two guards. His head was light from lack of food and his dry tongue stuck thick to the back of his mouth. He'd been falsely accused, and without Bessie to speak for him, there was nothing he could do to save himself. His stomach was a tight knot of rage and fear. He'd seen people hanged. It was an ugly death. And where was Bessie now? On her way to Marrakech? He tried to pray but he couldn't remember the words he'd learnt at the abbey. He squeezed his eyes shut and as he did, hot tears made tracks through the grime on his cheeks. How he longed for the safety of

Saint Wilfred's! *Please, God, get me out of this*, he prayed. *I'll do anything. I'll become a monk – take my vows. Only get me out of this!*

'This is the biggest hall in the land,' whispered Fustian to Bessie as he steered her under the great arched door of Westminster Hall. Gabriel Miller held his daughter firmly by the other arm, afraid that she might faint. 'This way to the King's Bench,' said Fustian. 'See that marble chair up on the raised platform? That's where the judge sits. The witness bench is below the dais.'

Bessie nodded. She could hardly speak. 'I pray this is going to work,' she said in a small voice. 'What if something goes wrong?'

'Have courage, Bessie,' whispered Fustian. 'I would trust Sir Ranulf de Lacy with my life.' Fustian glanced anxiously towards the door and as he did so, Sir Ranulf himself hurried in to join them, shaking the rain from his hair. He muttered a few quick words in Gabriel's ear and then together the group made their way to the witness bench at the front. Bessie didn't notice the boy with tousled black hair and eyebrows that met in the middle who glanced at them sideways as they passed down the hall, a dog held tight in his arms. Her eyes were fixed on something else which made her clutch her father's arm in fear. It was Jocelyn de Maltby, standing a head taller than most of the assembled crowd.

'It's *him*,' she gasped, resisting the powerful urge to turn and flee from the hall. She might have known *he* would be here for the trial. She pulled her hood close round her face. 'What if he sees me?' she whispered. 'Do you think he knows I've escaped?'

But there was no time to worry about that. No sooner had they taken their places on the witness bench, than a sudden commotion behind the dais announced the arrival of Sir Percy FitzNigel, and everyone's attention was turned on the Justice in his golden skull cap and flowing lawyer's gown. Sir Percy struck an attitude in the doorway casting his eyes over the throng of people with the expression of someone used to causing a stir. His nostrils flared as if he could discern a putrid smell.

For a moment his eyes rested on Sir Ranulf and an expression of relief crossed his face. Then his glance passed over the closely hooded figure of Bessie at Gabriel's side and alighted on the figure of Sir Jocelyn de Maltby. Their eyes met in silent communication, like old rogues well practised in reading each other's minds, and then in an extravagant whirl of robes, the King's Justice mounted the platform. A ragged silence fell, broken only by the flutter of a pigeon trapped somewhere high up in the rafters. The Justice licked his lips and, with a self-important cough, reached down to take a roll of parchment from his clerk. Bessie was alternately biting her nails and taking deep breaths – trying to keep herself calm. She twisted round in her seat, staring anxiously back towards the door over the heads of the people behind.

'We are gathered today,' began the King's Justice in a cold clear voice, 'in an extraordinary session of the King's Bench to bring before the court a most violent offender, a novice monk no less, who prompted by the devil, did commit three scandalous and wicked crimes. Namely, kidnapping a maid against her will, thievery of a precious relic from his abbey and attempted murder of his abbot, for any one of which he should deservedly hang by the neck until he be dead according to the ancient laws of this realm.'

A ripple of excitement ran through the assembled company, with cries of 'Shame! Hang the rascal! Bring him on!'

Rage gathered the corners of Bessie's mouth. She bit hard on her lip. It took all her self-control not to jump up and cry out. She glanced at Sir Ranulf. He was sitting forward on the bench, his rigid jaw set and his beard jutting forward. She looked fearfully behind her again but the great oak doors at the end of the hall remained shut. Her father's rough hand closed tensely over hers and she twisted her palm and laced her fingers tightly within his. 'Courage, Bessie,' whispered Gabriel.

Sir Percy FitzNigel lifted his eyes from the parchment. 'In a moment I shall call upon the witnesses here present to come to the bar to tell what they have personally seen or heard.' He looked up, his hard green glare alighting on Sir Ranulf de Lacy and Gabriel Miller. 'But before I do, I will call upon the guards to bring forth the prisoner!'

Bessie felt she might faint. The door behind the dais was opening. Any moment now and she would see Tom . . .

Outside Westminster Hall the cobbles in the yard shone slick with rain as the cart carrying the Lord Chief Justice bumped and rattled towards the great oaken doors where the soldiers from Westminster Palace waited in accordance with their orders.

'This is most unwise, Sir Henry,' fussed his physician, his face creased with concern. 'You have not the strength. Pray let us return home. It is not too late to send somebody else.'

Sir Henry's face was pale, his bloodless lips pressed tight with pain, but his eyes were aflame. 'I will see to this matter myself if I die in the attempt,' he spat, his eyes gleaming. 'That a fellow lawyer and Justice to the King could sink so low! I never liked the devil but *this*!' he spluttered. '*This* is monstrous!'

Back inside the courtroom, Bessie couldn't help herself. At the sight of Tom, his hands shackled and his filthy face a mask of terror, she sprang to her feet with a cry of anguish, her hood falling back from her face. Tom's head shot up. He'd know the sound of that cry anywhere.

'Silence!' cried Sir Percy, glancing enquiringly at Sir Jocelyn whose back had suddenly stiffened. The knight was staring at Bessie, the shock of recognition rippling over his face. At that same moment, the great banded doors of the Court of Justice swung open and the Lord Chief Justice limped in, leaning heavily on his crooked stick, flanked by the palace guards.

A look of annoyance passed over Sir Percy's face. 'What is this disturbance?' he asked irritably as the Lord Chief Justice hobbled down the hall. 'The court is in session! Witnesses to the bar!' he commanded. 'In the name of the King, I call Sir Ranulf de Lacy!'

But Sir Ranulf stood rooted to the spot looking towards

Sir Henry de Mandeville who had almost reached the table where the clerk sat hunched over his papers, quill suspended in mid-air. A profound silence fell over the hall, the only sound the tramp of the soldiers' boots and the sharp tap tap of the Chief Justice's walking cane. A tremor of expectation passed through the crowd.

Sir Henry de Mandeville, the Lord Chief Justice of England, raised his cane. Sir Percy frowned. Something was wrong! Sir Henry's voice was weak but the note of menace was unmistakeable. 'Sir Percy FitzNigel! I arrest you in the name of the King for the murder of Brother Gideon, sacrist of Westminster Abbey!'

Sir Percy flinched, the colour rushing to his face. A convulsive quiver ran through his elegant body. He glanced wildly about him. How could this be? Who had betrayed him? The palace guards were moving towards him now, their hands on their swords. He caught Sir Jocelyn's eye. The knight had risen to his feet and was edging discreetly through the crowd nearest the dais. The Lord Chief Justice saw him out of the corner of his eye. 'Seize that man too,' cried Sir Henry de Mandeville. 'The knight with the silver finger!'

Sir Jocelyn de Maltby shot Percy a frantic look. Their eyes locked for a moment, and then Sir Jocelyn jerked his chin towards the door behind the King's Bench. It was the slightest of movements but one that Sir Percy readily understood. It would be hard to sprint in his lawyer's robes. Swiftly, he let the smooth fabric drop from his shoulders, like a snake shedding its skin. The robes swished to the ground, a froth of silk around his knees, and then with a leap he jumped from the dais and was running towards the door, Jocelyn de Maltby hard on his heels.

'Stop those men, you fools!' cried Sir Henry to the guards. 'Stop them, in the name of the King!'

Chapter 29

Most Dangerous Game in London

The rain had turned the snow to slush as Percy and Jocelyn fled from the back of Westminster Hall and out onto the slippery riverbank. Percy had shot the bolt behind them and they could hear the soldiers, hammering on the door. Great drops of rain like silver pennies peppered the choppy surface of the river. Percy and Jocelyn planned breathlessly as they ran. There was only one thing on their minds. Escape! Preferably with the casket. FitzNigel Hall was near. It was risking their necks to go there but greed had always been their master and without the casket all this would have been for nothing. A horn sounded somewhere on the other side of Westminster Hall. 'God's blood!' swore Jocelyn. 'They've raised the hue and cry!'

'Thank God I barred the door!' panted Percy. 'It's given

us a chance at least. Quick, follow me. There's a row boat tied up at the jetty. Is *Los Tres Magos* still moored at Queen's Hythe?'

Sir Jocelyn nodded. 'If we can get the casket and then make for the row boat without being seen,' he said, 'with the tide on the turn . . .'

'We'll be aboard *Los Tres Magos* before you can say Three Wise Men!'

But Sir Jocelyn was in no mood for jokes. 'We've not got away with this one yet, Balthazar,' he snarled.

Nor had they. For as the two figures crept stealthily towards FitzNigel Hall, three soldiers appeared at a run. They huddled together as if to confer, and then one made off west back towards the Palace of Justice and the other two turned eastwards in the direction of FitzNigel Hall.

Sir Percy's house was in darkness. No candles were lit and only a feeble fire smouldered in the stone hearth. 'Watch the window, Melchior,' ordered Percy, 'and I'll get the chest.' He glanced regretfully around at the sumptuous room. *It was too bad to be leaving all this behind – just when things were going so well.*

Sir Jocelyn turned from the window in agitation. 'What are you waiting for, Balthazar?' he hissed. 'Don't just stand there! Fetch the casket! I value my neck even if you care nothing for yours!'

But Percy did care for his – very much – and a few moments later, the two men were creeping furtively out of the garden entrance, retracing their steps down towards the river, just as the soldiers leading the hue and cry surged into the cobbled courtyard of FitzNigel Hall. With curses and shouts, they swarmed up the broad stone steps flanked by stone lions and hammered on the iron-studded door with three crowns on its coat of arms.

Back in the courtroom Bessie had sprung to Tom's side. Seizing his hands, she pulled desperately at the manacles that bound him. 'Thank God Sir Henry made it in time. I nearly died of the tension!' She stared up at Tom, tears in her eyes, but Tom had not moved. He stood rigid, his face a mixture of confusion and relief. The Lord Chief Justice was slumped on a bench, supported by Sir Ranulf de Lacy who had broken his fall as he'd tottered to the ground in a swoon.

His physician fluttered around him in his black robe, like a crow around its fledgling. 'I said this would prove too much for him in his weakened state of health,' he fussed. 'He should have sent somebody else!'

Bessie made an impatient sound in her throat. She looked desperately from the gaolers to Sir Henry and back to the gaolers again. 'Hasn't anyone got the key to these manacles?' she cried, stamping her foot. 'Don't worry, Tom,' she said. 'We'll have you free in no time.' But Tom didn't seem to hear. He was staring down the hall, an expression of hurt in his eyes. A dark haired boy was scurrying towards the great ribbed door at the opposite end of the hall. Without a backward glance, Bart slipped unnoticed out into the rain, a bundle of grubby white fur clutched tightly under his arm.

* * *

The sturdy rowing boat rocked with the swell of the tide at the foot of the water stairs. The wind had risen and there was a rumble of thunder in the air as gulls flew bright white against the leaden sky. 'Thank God for the turn in the tide,' said Sir Jocelyn as he stepped heavily into the boat, lurching sideways as an unexpected wave slammed the craft to the end of its mooring chain with a clatter. 'But God *damn* this wind,' he cursed, seizing the chain and reeling the boat in for Sir Percy to clamber aboard, the green leather pouch held tight in his hands.

Percy peered through the driving rain. 'On an ebb tide we'll reach Queen's Hythe in no time at all,' he said breathlessly, bending over to tuck the casket under a coiled rope in the prow. 'We've done well, Melchior. Once on *Los Tres Magos* our troubles will be over. Now cast off this row boat and I'll take the oars!'

Out in the middle of the river a damp mist seethed and wound itself about the boat. Percy pulled hard on the oars and the wind blew the spindrift in their faces. As Sir Jocelyn crouched in the stern, his cloak flapping, he was thankful to see the city of Westminster rapidly receding, shrouded in a ghostly mist. He blew out his cheeks, starting to relax for the first time. Then suddenly Sir Jocelyn started, leaning out with his hands on the stern and peering upriver through the slanting rain. A boat with a lantern was following behind them, rather too close for comfort. He could see the yellow light and hear the splash of oars as the surging tide carried them rapidly downriver. 'There's a boat behind us!' hissed Sir Jocelyn, an edge of panic in his voice. 'It's a way off yet but we're being followed . . . and it looks like soldiers!'

And then they heard the cry, echoing through the sheeting rain. 'Stop! Stop in the name of the King!' A cacophony of voices took up the same cry. And then they saw more boats behind the first, lantern lights bobbing on the grey water. The hue and cry had taken to the river.

There was no other choice but to row, harder than they'd ever rowed in their lives. On and on the fugitives ploughed, taking turns on the oars, the one not rowing using the paddle, past Whitehall Stairs and around the great bow bend of the river, sometimes stretching more river between themselves and the following boats and sometimes less. In spite of the bitter wind, Sir Jocelyn had cast off his fur-trimmed cloak, his face perspiring with the effort, even though they were running with the tide.

A tense silence had fallen between the two men, each lost in his own thoughts and intent on the job in hand. They had just passed Puddle Wharf and in the distance they could see London Bridge with its nineteen arches spanning the river. They would soon be at Queen's Hythe. They would make it before their pursuers, jump ashore and hoist the sails of *Los Tres Magos*. There would be no stopping them in this wind. Then they would be free!

It was the sight of the bridge that reminded Sir Jocelyn of something that made the blood freeze in his veins. He cried out, slapping his forehead with the flat of his hand. 'The bridge! God Bones! The bridge! What fools we are. This isn't going to work.' Sir Percy stared at him, bewildered. 'The bridge, you fool,' snapped Jocelyn. 'The drawbridge is down!'

The drawbridge was raised twice daily on the incoming

tide to allow the bigger ships through to the western wharfs. But now the tide had turned and the bridge would be closed. What they had thought was a blessing now became a curse. *Los Tres Magos* was a small-masted cog, but nonetheless her mast was too tall. They could never sail her underneath the bridge unless the drawbridge was up.

Sweat broke out afresh on Percy FitzNigel's brow. He glanced back, a panic-stricken look on his face. Their pursuers were still there, sometimes gaining on them, sometimes dropping back. The two wise men stared at each other, realisation washing over them like a wave of cold spume.

Sir Jocelyn's mind was racing. Maybe there was just one chance. He narrowed his eyes at the rapidly approaching bridge. He'd seen experienced watermen 'shoot the bridge' in rowing boats and lose their lives, smashed to their deaths on the great stone pillars or sucked beneath the boiling water. It was the most dangerous game in London. No one but a fool ever rowed under London Bridge, even on a calm day. And with a wind like this and the river full of melting snow, the water would be churning like the devil's cauldron.

Sir Percy's face was white as the foam on the water. 'We're trapped,' he wailed. 'The water's already starting to seethe and we're way upstream of the bridge. We can't go back and we can't go on!'

Sir Jocelyn curled his narrow lip in an expression of contempt. 'So what do you suggest, Balthazar? That we give ourselves up to the hue and cry? Or perhaps you'd prefer us to swim!'

Sir Percy's hands flew to his face in a spasm of despair.

'So what . . . what are we going to do?' he gibbered. 'You're not suggesting we shoot the bridge?'

A grim smile played around Sir Jocelyn's lips. 'Well none of our pursuers would dare,' he said softly. 'The drop in the water level from one side to the other at high tide is the height of a man. You are right, Balthazar. We are indeed trapped . . . between the hangman's noose and a watery death under London Bridge!' He peered through the mist at the steadily advancing craft behind them. 'You may swim for the shore if you wish. Jump out now with my blessing. But that will guarantee you the gallows. I for my part have nothing to lose and everything to gain. I intend to shoot the bridge. I will stake my life on the most dangerous game in London.'

A crowd had gathered on London Bridge. Word had spread like a forest fire and now eager people jostled and shoved for the best viewing point of the drama unfolding upstream. Tier upon tier of faces peered over the parapet between the crooked houses that hung over the seething water below.

'They'll be smashed to pieces!'

'They'll need the luck of the devil!'

'God help the poor fools!'

As Sir Jocelyn had predicted, the boats full of soldiers were hanging back, sculling their oars, looking on in growing disbelief. Others were rowing for the riverbank. Surely only a fool would shoot the bridge on a day like this. Even the most experienced watermen would baulk at the idea.

Between the arches the water raged white where the

force of the current met the partial damn, turning the river into a furious cascade of spray and spume. High up on the bridge, faces were pressed to windows and some daring youths had even clambered out onto a wooden crane to balance precariously above the raging torrent and get a better view. As the Two Wise Men neared the bridge the river roared under their hull, spray flying in their faces as rolling waves smashed into the side of the little craft. Sir Percy sat rigid in the prow, his knuckles bone-white on the rim of the boat, paralysed with fear.

'Do something, you fool!' roared Sir Jocelyn. He had urged Sir Percy to take an oar, a weapon in case they missed their mark and slammed into the solid stone pillars, but Percy's nerve had failed him at the last. Quivering like a kitten, he crouched in the bow whilst Sir Jocelyn, oar in hand, prepared for the onslaught. 'De Maltby always has the last laugh,' he muttered, slinging the casket around his neck, safe in its crocodile-skin bag.

As the boat nudged forward, a deathly hush fell over the crowd. Sir Jocelyn de Maltby stood in the prow, legs braced, his unblinking eyes fixed on the central arch of the bridge. Then all at once the boat shuddered; then plunged. And suddenly there was a monstrous sucking sound. Sir Percy screamed, his arms flailing as the boat reared up on its stern. Then, as the river took possession of its prey, the crowd erupted in one loud and furious roar.

Plunging down again the boat began to spin, faster and faster like a fairground top. The river heaved, forcing them upwards in a torrent of water. And all at once they were flying under the bridge.

Spray stung their eyes.

They couldn't see.

They couldn't breathe.

There was a booming noise that filled the whole arch and then in front of them, a solid grey wall of water.

Sir Jocelyn stabbed with his oar, trying to keep the boat from smashing into the stone arch but it splintered like matchwood in his hands.

They were in the boat.

They were out of the boat. Sir Jocelyn was trapped underneath its upturned hull. Sir Percy's face slammed against a stone pillar and then he was lurching away, arms outstretched, as if he were flying through the water.

As the small boat disappeared under the bridge, the crowd surged to the other side, clawing each other and trampling toes in their eagerness to witness the sight downstream. On this side the raging water thundered through the arches like nineteen plunging waterfalls as the height of the river dropped full six feet into a whirlpool of foam. On a successful shoot, the boat would explode like a bung from a fermenting bottle . . . but of Percy FitzNigel and Jocelyn de Maltby, there was no sign.

Later that day when the tide had run out, a fur-lined cloak was found ripped into tatters, forlornly dangling from a stony outcrop under the bridge. Below it on a muddy ledge lay the golden buckle of an elegant shoe . . . all that was left of the King's Justice and The Man with the Silver Finger.

Chapter 30

Farewell Bart and Flea

It was the morning of the following day and although Tom and Bessie agreed that they had never slept better, they were both still tired beyond speech. Gabriel Miller had already packed their saddlebags. He was anxious to get home to Alice and set her mind at ease. He couldn't rest with the knowledge that his wife remained beside herself with fear.

It was still raining and the streets were ankle deep in slush as the hard-packed snow continued to melt. Sir Ranulf had ridden out early to bid farewell to his old friend the Lord Chief Justice who he'd found sitting up in bed and taking a little camomile tea, already feeling better for not breakfasting on barley bread and honey. Fustian had been out early too, visiting the apothecary in Crooked Lane and had come back with a number of little packages to attend to Tom's wounds – a poppy infusion for his headache and a nettle poultice for his wrists and ankles, still raw from the Newgate manacles. Tom had a lump on the back of his head the size of a gull's egg. So no one was more surprised than Fustian when Tom announced he had an important errand on London Bridge.

'It will only take a few minutes,' promised Tom. 'It's something I have to do. Sir Ranulf's coming with me. We'll set off for home just as soon as I'm back.'

Tom felt shy on his own with Sir Ranulf de Lacy, and the baron did his best to set him at ease, chatting amiably as they squelched through the muddy slush of Fish Street Hill and down onto London Bridge.

'Poor Sir Henry de Mandeville is still in shock, and who wouldn't be?' said Sir Ranulf in his usual jovial fashion. 'To discover that one of your Justices is guilty of murder is one thing, but to find that the devil was trying to poison you and wooing your daughter at the same time is quite another!'

Tom nodded but he didn't smile. Somehow he didn't feel the kind of happiness he ought and he suspected Bessie felt the same way.

There was still a holiday atmosphere in the streets. There was a fortune teller on the bridge, promising health and happiness in return for a quarter penny and the same mangy bear Tom had seen before, dancing miserably on its chain.

'We're here,' said Tom, coming to a halt between the pastry shop and the rope maker's. 'If you don't mind waiting outside, Sir Ranulf, I'll only be a moment.'

The broken shutters were closed. Tom peered through a jagged hole into the hovel that Bart called home. There

228

was part of Tom that hoped he wasn't in and yet another part of him couldn't rest until he had seen Bart and asked him why. He'd thought of Bart as a friend. How could he have been so wrong?

The room looked empty but as Tom stared he noticed a mound in the corner next to a tiny fire. A boy and a dog lay sound asleep, their limbs so entwined that it was impossible to see where the boy ended and the dog began. Tom pushed open the door.

'Who's that?' cried Bart, heaving himself up on his elbow as a slice of daylight fell on his face. And then Tom was hit by a thunderbolt of fur and a lashing tongue as Flea leapt ecstatically into his arms.

'Oh, it's you.' Bart said sulkily. 'What do you want?'

Tom placed a struggling Flea down on the floor. The little dog sat on his feet gazing up at him, panting with pleasure. Tom swallowed. 'You betrayed me,' he said in an unsteady voice. 'I trusted you. I thought we were friends.' He bent down sadly and stroked the dog's matted fur.

Bart glowered at Tom from under his black brows. '*Friends*,' he sneered. 'What are friends?'

Tom frowned. 'Well, at the abbey when you've got a friend you . . .'

'Oh stuff you and your abbey,' Bart scoffed cutting him short. 'It made me wild inside when I heard you talk about it. You felt so sorry for yourself having to take your vows an' all that and yet you've got clothes on yer back and food in yer belly and an abbot you say is like a father. Don't sound too bad to me. You don't know when you're well off, you don't!'

Tom shifted awkwardly. Somehow he didn't hate Bart for what he had done. He supposed the boy had to use every trick he could. Just to survive. And at least he'd helped Bessie in the end . . . nevertheless, Tom felt betrayed.

He looked around at Bart's hovel, at the bucket full of coloured water that his orphaned sisters used for dying the crucifixes, and at the rags at the mean little window. 'I might have been hanged,' he said softly.

'Yeah well.' And now it was Bart's turn to look awkward. 'I didn't know you at first, did I? I was sent by Sir Percy to watch for *Los Tres Magos* comin' in on Christmas Day. When the boat moored up I was to run an' tell him it had docked. I saw Sir Jocelyn an' the girl come off an' then whilst I was finishin' off me tankard of ale I saw you emerge from behind a barrel. Who's this, I said to meself? So I waited for you to come ashore and followed you. I just introduced meself when you was passin' *The Dog's Head Tavern*. All I did was tell Sir Percy about you.'

'And arrange for me to be captured in *The Three Cripples Inn*,' spluttered Tom, 'and locked up in Sir Percy's house! And then when I escaped you tipped off my pursuers and then gave me the wrong directions to *The Mule Inn*, so I got banged up in Newgate Prison!'

Bart wrinkled his nose. 'You don't know nuffink about my life, you don't,' he said shaking his head. 'No mother an' father and them two little girls to look after. I'll tell you me Dad's golden rule, for what it's worth. It's what he used to say to me before he was hanged. "You look out for yourself, Bart, 'cos there ain't no one else who's gonna do it for you!" Sir Percy paid me well for me trouble. Now what am I gonna do for money? Besides, I saw your friend Bessie right, didn't I?'

For a moment Tom held Bart's gaze and then gave a curt little nod. Bart was right. If it hadn't been for his lock-picking skills she might be on her way to Africa now. Tom sighed, fumbled in his jerkin and brought out a small leather pouch, heavy with silver coins. 'Speaking of Bessie, this is for you,' he said awkwardly. 'It's from her father – to say thank you for helping her.'

Bart glanced briefly at the purse but he didn't take it. 'It's just that you don't understand how good you've got it, that's all,' he said with a frown. 'You don't know what a really tough life is.' He looked up sadly. 'You're not so bad really – but it's too late now to be friends.'

There was a scuffle outside the door and a moment later Martha walked in, little Meg on her back and her arms full of washing. 'Bart! Bart!' called little Meg. Martha bent down to let the little girl slide off and she ran to Bart, wrapping her arms round his head and pressing her cheek against his.

Tom smiled a greeting at Martha and then his eyes wandered wistfully to Bart and little Meg on the floor. He swallowed. *At least Bart has a real family*, he thought. *My father dumped me at the abbey doors. Maybe Bart should know when he was well off too.*

'I'd better be going,' said Tom, putting the leather pouch on the barrel that served as a table. 'Sir Ranulf de Lacy's waiting for me outside.'

Bart gave a crooked little smile. 'That's what I mean,' he said with a shrug. He put on a voice to imitate Tom. '"Sir

Ranulf's waiting for me!" It's all right for the likes of you. You'll always get looked after.' Bart got up, disentangled himself from little Meg and gathered Flea into his arms. There was a silence.

'Goodbye, Bart,' said Tom, turning sadly on his heel. 'Look after Flea. He's a great little dog.'

'Don't you worry about me,' Bart called as the hovel door banged shut behind Tom. 'Me and Flea'll be all right!'

Chapter 31

Mudlarks

Due east of London Bridge, the river lapped against the water gate at the foot of the Tower of London. The tide was low, and the mudlarks' feet sank deep into the grey-green mud of the river bank. These were the scavengers, the lowest of the low-life of the city, who kept starvation at bay by searching the weed-slicked rubble. Bent double, seaweed popping underfoot, they crawled like insects over the slimy rocks, their faces nearly level with the sludge as they groped in shallow pools and delved their crooked fingers into the crevices between rocks. On a good day, they would fill their broken baskets with river shrimps and gritty cockles, and once in a while they'd find a corpse with a golden ring.

'Any luck, Noah?' said the bent old woman in a cracked voice.

'Nah. Nuffink, Liza. There ain't even any whelks today,' he said, reaching a skinny arm between two rocks up to the shoulder and splaying out his fingers to grope in the slime. He frowned, then wiggling his arm out, he pushed it in again at a different angle. 'Hold on a minute, though. What we got 'ere?'

It was a small sack, sodden with river water and made of a kind of leather – but not from any animal old Noah had ever seen. The woman scuttled crab-wise across the freezing mud. Noah delved into the bag, his eyes eager with expectation. 'Lord, save us!' he whispered as the golden casket slid from the sack. 'Pinch me, Liza. 'cos if you don't, I'll think I've died and gone to 'eaven!'

Liza gazed at the casket. 'It looks like one of them relics they've got in the great abbey at Westminster – what all them pilgrims pay to touch.'

It was mid-afternoon and yet the light was already failing. Abbot Swithin sat in the choir stalls at Westminster Abbey, looking up at the soaring arches. He was quite alone. Or at least he was now, having just seen off the constable and the sheriff who had brought a cart for the body of Brother Gideon. It was about time too. The body had lain full seven days in the crypt and even in this winter weather the smell had begun to creep up from the undercroft. He would need to arrange the funeral now that the sheriff was back and the mystery of his sacrist's death resolved. He'd never liked Brother Gideon, but the things he had learnt since his death had come as a great surprise. To think that one of his own monks had forged a degree from the University of Paris! He closed his eyes and imagined the relic that had just slipped through his fingers – the golden casket that the Magi had brought to Bethlehem! Of course, Cologne Cathedral had the bodies of The Three Kings and he could never have rivalled that, but even so – the casket would have brought the pilgrims flocking to Westminster . . . and glory to the name of Abbot Swithin. He sighed. But he could never have kept it anyway. Not once hc knew where it had come from.

He looked up, his attention caught by a half-remembered scent, pungent and exotic, and the swirl of a cinnamon robe. The high priest of Zarathustra was treading softly down the nave, picking his way carefully between the puddles, his dark skin gleaming in the candlelight. He held up his long-fingered hand as Abbot Swithin began to rise.

'Pray do not get up, Abbot. You look tired. I came simply to say goodbye. I leave on the evening tide on a ship bound for Flanders. And from there I will return to my own temple in Persia with a heavy heart. Our precious casket is gone and it seems that my fellow priests died in vain – may Ahuru Mazda bless their souls.'

Abbot Swithin nodded. 'I am sorry for you. I wish there was something I could do to help.'

The priest smiled a sad smile, fingering the three knots on the cord around his waist. 'Good thoughts, good words, good deeds,' he murmured. 'That is what the great prophet Zarathustra taught and it is all we can do on this earth. You are a good man, Abbot Swithin. I pray that the great Ahuru Mazda will give you his blessing.' He turned at a noise behind him. A filthy old man in crimson britches was making his way up the nave of Westminster Abbey followed by a woman in a shabby mud-stained skirt. Abbot

Swithin rose to his feet, an enquiring look on his face, and went to stand beside the priest of Zarathustra.

The bent old man was carrying a drawstring bag in his hands.

'I was wonderin',' he said to Abbot Swithin, with a curious glance at the dark-skinned man, 'if you knew where we could find the Abbot of Westminster.' He jerked his head towards the woman by his side. 'Me and Liza – we've got somefink we'd like to show him . . .'

It was dusk on the second day of riding when Tom noticed the barren fields giving way to bleak hills, rising in folds of charcoal and grey from the valley of the River Twist. In the summer they were purple with heather and the air smelled of tansy and marjoram but today there was only the aroma of wood smoke, spiralling from the huddled villages. Away in the distance he could see the yellow monastery of Saint Wilfred's, its new tower rising amidst the scaffolding.

'The monks will be abed long before we arrive in Saint Agnes,' said Sir Ranulf. 'Tom had better stay with Fustian and me at Micklow Manor tonight. Then we can ride over in the morning to see Abbot Fergus and tell him all that has happened.'

Tom looked sadly at Sir Ranulf. Over the two-day journey he had come to feel a closeness with his companions that only shared adventures could bring. And now it was all over. He'd been away from the abbey for only a few days, and that freedom had been nothing short of terrifying. And yet now as they trotted towards the home of his boyhood, his stomach felt hollow with longing for something other than the cloistered life. He felt the blood rush to his cheeks as he remembered Bart's sneering words. *'You don't know when you're well off, you don't!'* And then with a shock he remembered how he'd prayed when he thought he would hang. *'Please God, get me out of this! I'll do anything. Take my vows, become a monk. Only get me out of this!'* When he thought he would hang he'd bargained with God. God had kept his side of the bargain and now the time had come for Tom to keep his.

Chapter 32

Inspiration

No one was more delighted to see Tom than Herbert, and though he had never really believed ill of Tom, he felt relieved that his faith in his friend had proved right after all. But although Tom tried hard at his friendship with Herbert, there was a new kind of distance between them; as if Herbert knew that things would never be quite the same, and that Tom was not as pleased to be home as Herbert wanted him to be.

Tom had only seen Bessie a couple of times since their return a week before, furtive meetings down by the frozen river or in the monk's burial ground behind the infirmary. But in these few snatched moments, Tom had told her about his promise on the day of the trial.

'Anyone would have said the same prayer in your position, Tom,' she said reassuringly. She was carrying a huge bunch of mistletoe in a cloth in her arms. 'It's what everyone does when they're frightened. Except pagans like me, who cast spells,' she grinned.

'And cut mistletoe without letting it touch the ground,' teased Tom glancing at the rough knife in her hand. 'I thought the Druids used to use a golden sickle.' He smiled but his eyes were sad. 'You really are a pagan, aren't you, Bessie?' He sighed. 'Anyway, what does it matter? I've spoken to Abbot Fergus again about not taking my vows. He was very understanding this time. He even admitted I wasn't cut out for the abbey. He said if I had rich parents he'd advise them to apprentice me to someone – but they gave no money when they left me at the abbey doors – and so there's no funds to buy me a trade.'

Bessie drew her black brows together. 'An apprentice?' she said slowly. 'What sort of apprentice?'

Tom shrugged. 'I don't know. A barrel maker or a carpenter. Anyway, it's not going to happen. Look, I must go. Brother Dunstan is on my back more than ever since all this happened and there'll be the devil to pay if I'm caught talking to you.'

'No, wait, Tom,' said Bessie, stamping her foot. 'There must be something we can do.' She stared angrily at the ground, biting her lip and then suddenly she gasped as if she'd had an idea.

'What's the matter?'

'Nothing. Nothing,' she said breathlessly, her eyes shining. 'I must go now. Will I see you tomorrow at the Twelfth Night revels?'

'Abbot Fergus says we can go if we want,' said Tom looking puzzled.

'Right then,' she said, backing away with a grin. 'I'll see you tomorrow.' And then in a swirl of her cloak, she was gone, running as fast as she could across the frosty grass towards Micklow Manor.

It was late afternoon on the fifth of January, the end of the twelve days of Christmas, and there was such excitement that the old tithe barn at Micklow Manor seemed to creak in its joints with anticipation. Bessie Miller glanced anxiously towards the door. She was busy with her mother, festooning the rafters with swags of fresh greenery: holly and mistletoe, bay and yew, as servants rolled barrels of ale into position at the farthest end. Tonight the workers from the estate would crunch through the frosty grass in the light of the twelve bonfires that would soon be lit on Fiddler's Hill, to take a slice of Twelfth Night cake with Sir Ranulf, the Lord of the Manor.

Bessie's fingers were numb with cold as she struggled to weave the mistletoe into a kissing bough. Her stomach felt full of snakes. She jumped as the barn door creaked open. *Please let it be Sir Ranulf back from the abbey*! But it was only Brother Ethelwig come to try out his new invention before tonight – the 'Decafluminator' – designed to light ten candles all at once.

In the outer court of Saint Wilfred's Abbey, Abbot Fergus stood with his hand on Sir Ranulf's bridle. It had begun to snow lightly, and his wild auburn hair around his tonsure was spangled with stars. Sir Ranulf leaned down and grasped his hand. A few more brief words and Sir Ranulf was wheeling his hunter around, setting off at a trot under the arch of the northern gate. Abbot Fergus took a deep breath to ease the ache of sadness in his throat. A small novice scurried across the courtyard, his grey woollen cowl pulled tight around his face.

'Ah, young Edmund,' said Abbot Fergus in an unsteady voice. 'Just the boy I need. Would you be so good as to fetch Brother Thomas for me? Ask him to come to the abbot's house right away.'

Tom walked quickly across the cloisters towards the abbot's house, racking his brains. He'd done everything he could to please the novice master these last few days so what was the problem this time? The door opened before Tom had chance to knock. Abbot Fergus must have been watching from the window.

'I can't think what I've done wrong this time,' Tom blurted as soon as the Abbot sat down. 'I can't please Brother Dunstan whatever I do!'

Abbot Fergus held up his hand. 'Peace, Tom. You have done nothing wrong,' he said gently. 'Quite the contrary. In fact I have a surprise for you. Something unexpected has happened.'

Tom felt a shiver of anticipation run from the nape of his neck down to the base of his spine. He couldn't think what it could be and yet there was something in the abbot's expression that made the blood rush to his cheeks.

'It seems you have caught the eye of our Lord of the Manor,' said the abbot. 'Sir Ranulf is very impressed with you – with your honesty and loyalty . . . and your bravery.'

241

He paused. 'And it appears that he has need of a squire.'

'A . . . a squire?' stammered Tom.

Abbot Fergus nodded. 'Yes, Tom. Sir Ranulf de Lacy has only just left the abbey. He has asked me to speak to you on his behalf . . . and to offer you the opportunity if you want it.'

Tom's head felt light. He was dizzy, sick, joyful – all at the same time. He tried to frown – to compose his face and pretend to be considering but he couldn't help it. A grin broke out from ear to ear and then all at once a terrible thought struck him and just as suddenly the sun went in. 'But what about the vow I told you about?' he said in a small voice. 'When I told God I'd become a monk if he saved me from the gallows?'

Abbot Fergus got slowly up from his chair and went to stand in front of Tom. 'An abbot is supposed to be a father to his monks,' he said. 'That is what the word abbot means. So I will give you the best advice that I can and then the decision is up to you.' He placed both hands on Tom's shoulders. 'There are many ways to serve God, and not all of us have a calling for this cloistered life. You do not have to be a monk to do good in the world. Look at Sir Ranulf de Lacy himself. He is a fair master to his tenant farmers and a kind overlord, full of good words and good deeds. Everyone is welcome at his feasts at Lammas and Harvest, Christmas and Twelfth Night. If you train as his squire, you could do worse than learn by his example. I do not think God would mind that.'

Tom swallowed. 'There's another problem too. What can I say to Herbert? We arrived at the abbey on the same day all those years ago. He's the kindest, most loyal friend I've ever had. We're like brothers. How can I abandon Herbert again?'

'*Abandon* him!' laughed Abbot Fergus indulgently. 'Really Tom! Not everyone finds Saint Wilfred's as stifling as you do. Don't you worry about Herbert. He will make a fine monk, mark my words. And there is no reason why you should not remain friends. Not in the same way of course. Your life will be very different now.' He looked searchingly at Tom. 'You must look for your own life, Tom, and I will help Herbert find his. Who knows? He might even be abbot one day!' He smiled and squeezed Tom's shoulder. 'I think you have made up your mind already,' he said. 'Say nothing to Herbert tonight. Leave the explaining to me.' And with that, Abbot Fergus pulled Tom towards him in a huge bear-like hug and when he let go there were tears in his eyes. 'God go with you, Tom. I will miss you,' he said softly. He paused, and then his eyes suddenly crinkled into a familiar grin. 'But then again,' he said punching Tom playfully in the stomach. 'Who needs a chief chorister with a broken voice?'

Epilogue
Persia – 1221

The Fire Temple

It is a soft balmy night and the air is silky and still. A silver eastern moon shines high in a sky of midnight blue, pricked with stars like diamonds. The air is full of music, tiny brass bells and piping flutes, and the heady perfume of cypress and myrtle. A crowd of men and women in flowing robes of saffron and cinnamon has gathered at the foot of an enormous staircase cut into a sandy cliff. Up and up it rises through four high terraces set about with lemon trees, until more than a thousand feet above the sandy plain below, it comes to an end at the steps of the fire temple of Zarathustra.

A silver bell rings, louder and shriller than all the rest and the crowd falls silent. A priest in a white robe is walking barefoot through the grove of cypress trees at the edge of the plain. His dark skin is dappled by moonlight and shadow and on his forehead there is a mark in the shape of a flame. In his hands he holds a golden casket inlaid with the same tiny silver flames. They seem to shine with a lustre all of their own and around the chest is wound a white cord of purest lamb's wool, three knots along its length and ending in a moonstone, fashioned in the shape of a tear. The crowd parts to allow the priest to pass through. On reaching the foot of the stairs he begins to climb and as he climbs a melodious singing reaches faintly down from the terraces, borne on a myrtle scented breeze. Up and up he climbs as the singing grows louder. He reaches the top of the staircase and turns to face the sea of saffron and cinnamon on the plain below.

Slowly he raises the small casket above his head as if offering it to the silver moon and then he turns back to the small bare altar and lays it gently down. Then taking a lighted brand, he kindles the sacred flame of the fire temple. It burns bright as a beacon, shining out over the Persian plain. A whisper passes through the crowd like the rustle of wind through trees and then the priest turns. He fingers the cord around his waist, his lips moving in silent prayer, and then he begins to descend the stairs.

Down on the plain one thousand feet below, someone is moving through the crowd with a torch, stopping to light the small cresset lamps that each person cups in his hand. One by one as the lamps are lit the people hold them up above their heads, so that instead of a sea of orange and golden robes, it appears to the priest that he is walking into a sea of fire.

SARAH MATTHIAS

Sarah Matthias is an exciting new author, with a unique talent for writing gripping historical mystery stories for children.

Sarah was born in Manchester and grew up in Bingley. After graduating from Oxford she worked first for the BBC and then as a barrister. She gave up full-time work to bring up her children – she has four – and wrote her first book, The Riddle of the Poisoned Monk, to read to them at bedtime. History is one of her major passions and she particularly enjoyed researching the recipes and herbal remedies that appear throughout her books.

Tom Fletcher and the Three Wise Men is the second outing for the young novice who first featured in *Tom Fletcher and the Angel of Death*.

You can visit her website at
www.sarahmatthias.co.uk

Other books from CATNIP *by Sarah Matthias*:

TOM FLETCHER AND THE ANGEL OF DEATH

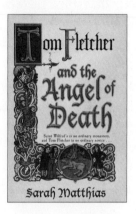

A beast house with a caged lion. A mad inventor devising the perfect flying machine. And a gruesome crime . . .

Saint Wilfred's is certainly no ordinary monastery. So it's just as well that 13-year-old Tom Fletcher is no ordinary novice.

When one of the monks is murdered in cold blood, and the wrong man accused of the crime, Tom has no choice but to turn detective. His investigation will put his own life at risk, and shake Saint Wilfred's to its foundations!

THE RIDDLE OF THE POISONED MONK

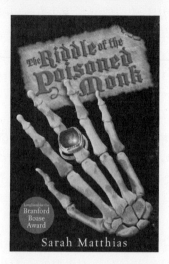

Charlie's mother is about to be taken for witchcraft,
Charlie too. With the aid of Balthazar, his cat, he
escapes – only to find himself in another time and a
different kind of danger!

In medieval Northumberland there are sinister
goings-on at Goslar Abbey. Someone is poisoning
the monks. In peril of his own life, can Charlie
decipher a runic riddle and solve the mystery?

A fast-paced tale of secrets, potions and
hidden treasure!

THE WIND EYE
by Robert Westall

Does a long-dead saint have the power to
destroy time itself?

On the sombre coast of Northumberland, near the
Farne Islands, a family holiday starts off with the
usual rows and bickering. Then, without warning,
strange things start to happen . . .

At the holiday home is a weird boat, like a
miniature Viking ship. The locals claim it
belongs to St Cuthbert – even though he died
over thirteen hundred years ago.

But when the boat takes the family back into
the past, to a time of violence and terror,
St Cuthbert – Cuddy – is the only one who
can help them. But will he?

*"A brilliant combination of the supernatural, family
conflicts and the bleak setting of the North East
coast"* Valerie Beirman

"A writer of rare talent" Michael Morpurgo

RAVEN BOY
by Pippa Goodhart

Legend has it that if the raven leaves the Tower of London, then monarch and kingdom will fall.

London 1666, the Great Plague rages and the city is a dangerous place. Young Nick Truelove blames his King, Charles II, for the hardships he faces, and vows to get revenge.

Inspired by the bold behaviour and wily cunning of a young raven, he bluffs his way into the centre of the King's power, the Tower of London itself.

But, as a remarkable friendship grows up between boy and raven, a new danger engulfs London. Nick's view of the world and his King is about to be changed for ever.

"This fast-moving adventure is a rich with historical detail: enjoyable and informative it paints a vivid picture of momentous historical events and their impact on ordinary people"
The Guardian

SHORTLISTED FOR THE STOCKTON CHILDREN'S BOOK AWARD